BAMBOO KINGDOM

RIVER OF SECRETS

BAMBOO KINGDOM

RIVER OF SECRETS

ERIN
HUNTER

HARPER
An Imprint of HarperCollinsPublishers

Special thanks to Rosie Best

Bamboo Kingdom #2: River of Secrets
Copyright © 2022 by Working Partners Ltd.
Series created by Working Partners Ltd.
Map art © 2021 by Virginia Allyn
Interior art © 2021 by Johanna Tarkela

Library of Congress Cataloging-in-Publication Data
Names: Hunter, Erin, author.
Title: River of secrets / Erin Hunter.
Description: First edition. | New York, NY : Harper, [2022] | Series: Bamboo kingdom ; #2 | Audience: Ages 8–12. | Audience: Grades 4–6. | Summary: "Three pandas must separate the truth from the lies they've been raised on in order to save their kingdom"—Provided by publisher.
Identifiers: LCCN 2021042691 | ISBN 978-0-06-302198-3 (trade bdg.)
Subjects: CYAC: Pandas—Fiction. | Fantasy. | LCGFT: Novels. | Fantasy fiction.
Classification: LCC PZ7.H916625 Rk 2022 | DDC [Fic]—dc23
LC record available at https://lccn.loc.gov/2021042691

Typography by Corina Lupp
22 23 24 25 26 PC/LSCH 10 9 8 7 6 5 4 3 2 1
❖
First Edition

For Rowan

DRAGON MOUNTAIN

THE NORTHERN FOREST

FEAST CLEARING

THE SOUTHERN FOREST

PROLOGUE

QUIETSHORE, A BLACK-NECKED CRANE, bobbed and soared on the currents of air that flowed over the peaks and valleys of the Bamboo Kingdom. His mate, Stillwater, touched her black wing tips to his as they flew.

It would be so good to return to their nest in the gentle shallows of the great river. The long summer was coming to an end, and the northern shoreline would be the perfect place for them to roost during the harsh mountain winter.

They followed the glittering stream of the river as it cut through the kingdom, over rapids and through thick forests, until finally Stillwater let out a gentle croak.

"We're almost there. Look, there's the waterfall. The mossy rocks will be just around this bend." She turned in the air, her keen eyes searching the banks for their nesting place. But as they turned the bend in the river, Quietshore looked down at the water and immediately knew something was wrong.

"Where are the rocks?" he called.

The nesting ground didn't look at all the way he remembered it. He and Stillwater had spent some time after the great flood looking for the perfect place to build their new nest. When they had flown away in the early spring, they had left behind a gentle slope to a shallow pool surrounded by mossy rocks, perfect for trapping small fish and staying protected from the river current. But now there was a much sharper drop from the land to the edge of the river. . . .

"Look!" Stillwater chirped, and went into a dive, landing on the mossy top of a high rock outcropping. Quietshore landed beside her and gasped. There on the top of the rock was their old nest: a comfortable circle of twigs, splintered bamboo, and moss. It took him a moment to understand. Why wasn't it in the water? But then he realized that the nest hadn't moved—the river had! "Quietshore," Stillwater breathed. "The floodwaters are finally receding!"

Quietshore hopped down the rocks toward the new edge of the river. Nearby, a gnarled tree that had been completely submerged now stuck up out of the water, dripping with algae. A thin bamboo sprout with a single bright green leaf was already growing out of the silt beside it. The sun shone down on it all, drying out the rocks and glittering on the surface of the river. Even the current seemed a little gentler than it had been. Other birds hopped curiously along the banks, pecking at the soft earth, while a pair of flying squirrels soared from branch to branch over their heads, chittering excitedly.

"This is wonderful," Stillwater crowed. "Things are finally going back to normal!"

They bent their heads together for a moment, then split up to look for the perfect place to build their new nest. Quietshore found a shady spot in the new shallows, where the current lapped against a large, smooth white rock. They fetched twigs and leaves and began to twine them together and build them up, layer by layer. A large carp flashed by, and Quietshore paused to watch it find its way between forests of river weeds.

Stillwater took the twig from his beak and slid it into place, then stepped into the nest and out again, looking over their work with a skillful eye. Quietshore cawed softly to himself and preened a loose feather from under his wing. She was so good at nest building. The red patch on the top of her head caught the light as she worked, its distinctive gingko-leaf shape gleaming in the bright sunshine.

He threaded the loose feather into the nest, then stepped a little farther into the water, feeling the peculiar new current lapping at his spindly legs. The river would always warn them if there was trouble coming, but right now it felt unsettled. It wasn't the terrible splashing of an approaching predator that he felt. It was the sense of great change, and more changes still to come. . . .

There was a small splash behind him, and he turned to see Stillwater standing beside the nest, the twig she'd been holding now bobbing in the water beside her.

Her beak was slightly open, and her normally sharp gaze seemed unfocused.

"Did you feel that?" she cooed faintly.

Quietshore focused on the feeling of the current, but there was no change. "Feel what?" he asked.

"Something was here." All the feathers along Stillwater's neck were puffing up, and she hopped from foot to foot anxiously. "Didn't you feel it? It felt like something . . . *breathed* on me." After a moment's pause, she strode out into the river, her footsteps splashing water against Quietshore's legs. He watched, perplexed, as his mate paced up and down in the shallows, startling another carp that had been lazing in a patch of sunlight.

"What's the matter?" Quietshore asked, his own neck feathers beginning to ruffle. "I didn't feel anything."

"I . . . I think . . . I have to go." Stillwater finally stopped pacing, and met Quietshore's eyes. "I'm so sorry."

"Go?" Quietshore didn't understand. "We just got here. But we can move the nest, if—"

"No, that's not it," Stillwater said. "The nest is perfect—it's me. I feel something . . . *calling* me. There's something I need to do." She splashed through the water to his side and pressed her neck to his. "I'll be back as soon as I can."

"Wait, Still—" Quietshore began, but Stillwater didn't wait. She took off in a single leap, scattering a sparkling trail of water droplets through the air behind her. With a few powerful flaps of her black-and-white wings, she vanished into the Northern Forest and was hidden by the waving leaves of the bamboo.

Quietshore shook himself and took off, flapping anxiously after her, but she was already gone, as if a strong breath of wind had carried her far away. He circled in the air, looking for any sign of his mate or the currents that bore her, but he found nothing.

What was happening? Where was she going? When would she come back?

Would she ever come back?

With a quiet crack, part of the nest below him suddenly came away from the pale rock where it had been wedged, and the whole thing began to float into the river. Quietshore gave a horrified squawk and flew after it, splashing down in the river and seizing it in his beak to try to drag it back to safety.

What's the point? Without Stillwater . . .

But he wouldn't let himself think like that.

She'll come back, and when she does, she'll have a lovely nest to return to. Our nest.

He wrestled with the bundle of twigs, trying desperately to save it, even though parts of the nest were already falling apart and drifting away. Finally he managed to get it back to the pale rock. But he needed something to wedge it into place.

Frantically he cast around until he saw something long and gleaming white just under the water, the same pale white as the rock. But when he dipped his beak into the water and plucked it out, it kept on coming, longer and longer, until he was holding something thin and curved.

It wasn't rock—it was bone.

Quietshore had seen enough predators with their prey in the mountains to know that this was a rib bone, one that had belonged to a much, much larger creature than a fish.

He put the bone down gingerly and looked around.

There were bones everywhere. Hundreds of them, sticking up from the mud or gleaming in the shallows. These must be the bones of the creatures who died in the flood.

There were so many. He had taken them for rocks, the same kind as the large pale stone where they had built their nest. . . .

He turned and slowly began to circle the large stone. Then he stopped, shuddering, as he saw the two large round crevices on the other side. Eye sockets, and a sharp row of teeth below them.

A shriek startled Quietshore as he stood, staring at the field of bones where he'd made his home. He instinctively leaped into the air and found himself climbing alongside a flock of plovers.

"Fly, fly, hurry!" they cheeped at him. "Predator!"

Quietshore banked away from them, turning in the air to circle over the shoreline, looking for whatever had startled the birds. He saw the flying squirrels hastily leaping from tree to tree, and a crowd of panicking pheasants scattering from a rock where they'd been sunning themselves. . . .

Then he saw what had scared them, and fear seized him. The predator climbed lightly down the hill, black and orange stripes rippling as it went, ignoring the panic it had caused. Its whiskers twitched and it sniffed the air as it reached the edge of the water and waded in, letting the water lap around its chest.

Even from high above, Quietshore could hear the growl that rumbled through the air around the tiger. It seemed to stare across the river, ears pricked and tail lashing in the water.

Quietshore didn't know what the predator was hunting, but he was glad it wasn't him.

Finally the tiger turned and headed back onto the shore.

As it passed, its tail brushed against the nest. It dislodged from the side of the skull once more, and Quietshore watched with a sinking feeling in his chest as his home, all he had left of his missing mate, was carried away on the river.

CHAPTER ONE

LEAF CLIMBED UP ONTO the top of a flat rock and pointed her muzzle toward the Dragon Mountain. It was still so far away, shimmering purple behind the haze of swirling cloud, but Leaf knew they would find their way there somehow. A burst of cold wind ruffled her fur and she shuddered, looking up at the rocky slope they would have to climb next, and at the snowbanks visible on the horizon.

She had come so far with her best friend, Dasher the red panda—they had climbed peak after peak, sheltered from sleet, and survived the worst earthquake Leaf had ever felt. They had followed the Great Dragon's trail, and even allied themselves with a tiger. And the tiger had led them here.

She turned and looked down into the space between the clump of trees on the side of the mountain, where Dasher was tearing leaves from the purple healing bamboo for Aunt Plum to eat. She was already getting better, the sickness retreating from her wound, though it seemed as if she would have a nasty scar.

Beside them, another young panda sat, holding the end of the bamboo for Dasher. She looked just like Leaf, except that she was better fed, her shape rounder and her fur a little sleeker. Rain Prosperhill, Leaf's sister.

Thank you, Great Dragon, Leaf thought. *For saving Plum from the attack of the white monster, and for bringing Rain and me together.*

She had always dreamed of crossing the river and finding her mother, and her sister. And now not only had Rain found *her*, but they knew they had a third sibling, a triplet, some- where in the Bamboo Kingdom.

And we're Dragon Speakers.

She believed what the tiger Shadowhunter had told her about her destiny, but it was still very, very strange. She had always assumed that the Dragon could hear pandas when they thanked it for their feasts and asked it for its help, but know- ing that the Dragon might speak *back* made her reconsider her words.

Thank you for helping us, she thought, gazing back up at the Dragon Mountain. *I will do everything I can to be a good Dragon Speaker and put things right in the Bamboo Kingdom.*

She hoped that was the right kind of thing to say.

"Rain, dear, tell me all about the Prosperhill pandas," Plum said, sitting up to prop her back against a tree. "How many of them are there? It sounds as if the bamboo is much more plentiful there."

"Yeah. Loads," Rain said. Plum and Leaf both looked at her expectantly, but she didn't seem to want to elaborate.

She's still taking all of this in, Leaf thought. She could understand why—Rain had been half drowned in the river, and when she'd woken up she was far from home, where a strange panda had told her that she was one of triplets, that the panda she called Mother wasn't her real mother, and that she was a Dragon Speaker. Leaf couldn't blame her sister for thinking all of this might be a strange dream.

"And . . . tell me again," Plum prompted, frowning. "About Sunset. Is there no way you could have been mistaken?"

Rain let out a contemptuous laugh. "What, you mean maybe I just *imagined* him holding me underwater?"

Plum looked hurt. "Not at all, dear. I just mean . . . I met him once, before the flood, and he was a kind, wise Dragon Speaker. He never gave me any cause to think he was a liar."

Rain cocked her head and scratched behind her ear. "Well—no offense, really—but every other panda on the Prosperhill thinks the same as you. They say he's wise because he's good at making up vague prophecies that can't help but come true, and they say he's kind because they've never seen him making bargains with the golden monkeys so they'll beat up defenseless cubs. They don't think about how his ideas don't make any sense; they just go along with it. They *want* to believe in him, so they just *do*. Even my mother! Even my best friend, Pebble . . ."

She trailed off, and her grumpy expression melted into sadness.

"We'll get to the bottom of it," Plum said gently. "I don't know what happened to him while he was missing, but we'll find out why he's changed like this."

"*If* that's what's happened," Rain muttered. "We don't know for certain he was *ever* a good panda. I don't care either way. I just need to stop him."

"Hey, that shouldn't be too hard," Dasher piped up. "Not when they find out that the *real* Dragon Speakers are here!"

Aunt Plum let out a thin, happy sigh. Her eyes met Leaf's, and Leaf felt a little embarrassed to see the reverence in her gaze. "My own Leaf," she said. "A Dragon Speaker—and the first ever to share that honor with her littermates. I couldn't be more proud of you, dear. Of both of you," she added, looking at Rain.

Rain had gone back to frowning.

"I know it's a lot," Leaf told her sister. "But Dasher's right— I know you want to go back and help your friends, but we have a duty now. And that duty will help us save them! We can challenge Sunset, and help the whole Bamboo Kingdom!"

"And I'll help you do it," said Plum. She got to her paws slowly. Leaf ran to her, putting her shoulder close so that Plum could lean on her, but Plum let out a small chuckle and pushed her away with her nose. "I'm strong enough to walk—thanks to Dasher and his healing bamboo," she added, turning and giving the little red panda a grateful lick behind the ear. "I know what you need to do next. We must go on to the Dragon

Mountain. All new Dragon Speakers make that journey, to perform the ritual and be accepted by the Dragon itself."

"What ritual?" Rain asked.

"No other panda knows what actually happens in the cave," Plum said. "That's between the Speaker and the Dragon. But it's something every Speaker must do."

"Then we'd better get going," Leaf said. "If you're sure you can walk." She looked at her aunt, wincing at the fresh slashing wounds that the white monster had left across her nose and down one side of her flank. They weren't deep, but they were still raw, the white fur around them stained brown from the blood.

"As long as we rest for the feasts, I'll be fine," said Plum. She took a few experimental steps, and then a few more. Leaf stayed close behind, just in case she stumbled, but after they had walked a few bear-lengths she relaxed. She turned to Rain.

Her sister hadn't moved. She was still sitting under one of the twisted pine trees, sniffing the air and frowning. When she saw Leaf looking at her, she got to her paws, but her steps were hesitant. She kicked aside a patch of fallen pine needles.

"I'm not sure about this," she said. "What if you're wrong? You'll have walked all the way to that mountain for nothing. You could die. You could freeze to death or be eaten by leopards or that tiger could come back—what if this whole thing is just some kind of plot to make sure you're weak and isolated before he comes back to eat you?"

Leaf wanted to tell Rain not to be silly, but she reminded herself again that Rain hadn't had as long to get used to any of this. "Shadowhunter's on our side, I promise," she said, directing this partly to Dasher, who had looked suddenly horrified at Rain's idea of a cunning tiger scheme. "We'll be okay, if we stick together. And if we get to the Dragon Mountain and nothing happens, well, either way we'll know for sure, won't we?"

Rain sighed, and turned to look over her shoulder. Leaf followed her gaze and realized she was looking south, down the slope of the mountain toward the river and the Prosper-hill. She prepared to keep making her argument to Rain, but before she could, Rain looked away again.

"All right. I'll go with you. I guess I'll find out for certain that I'm no Dragon Speaker after all," she added with a grin. Leaf grinned back.

You're teasing me. Like a real sister!

As the four of them set off from the clearing to walk the rocky slope up toward the purple, mist-wreathed Dragon Mountain, Leaf's heart swelled. When they got to the Dragon's cave . . . what would happen? Would they see the Dragon for real? Would it speak to them?

Whatever it was, for now she was content to be walking toward it. She was with her sister, and soon enough Rain would accept it, too.

CHAPTER TWO

GHOST CLAWED AT HIS meal, trying to hold it down just like Winter had taught him, so he could get a clean killing bite. But the thing just wouldn't keep still—it flexed and wiggled even though he had it pinned, its waving arms getting in his face and making him rear back, which meant he lost his grip, which meant he had to pounce all over again.

"You can do it," Shiver cheered from her comfortable spot on a sunny rock nearby. Her eyes were dark as she followed the motion of his prey, and her fluffy tail twitched. "Get it!"

"You nearly had it that time," called another voice, from much farther away. Ghost tried to keep a firm grip on the food as he looked up and peered across the wide river to the panda who had called out to him from the opposite bank. His new friend Sunset Deepwood had shouted instructions to him about how to find food in this strange, warm, wet place. He said this prey would be worth the effort, but Ghost wasn't sure he believed it.

Sure enough, the strange, springy green plant that Sunset had called *bamboo* sprang out of his paws once again, whipping up to smack Ghost in the face. He reared back, shaking his head.

"Grab it with your jaws," Sunset shouted. "Near the root!"

Ghost took a deep breath. Perhaps he had been thinking of this all wrong, chasing after the waving leaves at the bouncy end. He worked his muzzle into the base of the stand, trying to ignore the way the shoots tickled his nose, and bit down on a bamboo cane. It came away almost at once, with a satisfying snap.

As soon as the scent of the cool green insides of the bamboo hit his nostrils, Ghost understood what Sunset had been talking about. It smelled fresh and slightly sweet, nothing at all like any of the prey he had eaten in the mountains. It smelled *delicious*.

He gripped it in his jaws and crunched down, splitting the bamboo cane open. It was a struggle to tear the strips of outer bark away, but it was worth it to get to the tasty green flesh inside. He pinned the cane down and worked his teeth into it, tearing at the bark with his claws.

"This is amazing!" he shouted back to Sunset, looking up with his mouth full of stringy bamboo.

"I'm glad you think so," Sunset replied. "But there's a much easier way to get to it, young Ghost."

He began to explain the best way to eat the bamboo, and Ghost stopped attacking it, puzzled by the fiddly-sounding instructions. He followed Sunset's direction and sat down on his haunches, instead of crouching over his prey like a leopard would. He used the grip pads on his paws to hold the bamboo, and then picked off the leaves with his teeth. He bundled them together and took a bite, and then almost laughed out loud at the wonderful taste—it was a different scent and texture from the inside of the cane, but just as delicious. He looked up at the waving leaves on the other canes still growing in the ground, and thought that he could happily sit here all day just munching on them.

"Can I try some?" Shiver jumped down from her rock and padded over to him. He held out a leaf, and she sniffed it carefully before picking it up in her teeth and chewing.

Her lips pulled back and her eyes squinted and rolled back in her head.

"Oh! It's just . . . ew!" She shook herself, trying to spit out the leaf. "It's just a plant!" The look on her face was so funny that Ghost couldn't help chortling at her, and after a disgusted snort, she joined in with Ghost's laughter. She started cleaning her paws, trying to get the taste out of her mouth, still chuckling to herself. Ghost was so glad to see her happy. They hadn't laughed like this since before . . .

All at once, the scene flashed before his eyes again: Winter, their mother, falling from the ledge. In his memory, the fall seemed to grow longer and longer, so that the snow leopard was falling through the air for an impossibly long time before she hit the bottom of the Endless Maw and lay still, never to move again.

He tried to shake off the image and focus on Shiver. She was still teasing, making a big fuss about how horrible she thought the bamboo was.

"All the more for me, then!" he said, forcing himself to smile as he dramatically lifted the cane away from her.

He was so glad to have his sister with him. He would have missed her so much if she'd let him leave the mountain alone. She had shown no sign of blaming him for Winter's death, the way their other littermates had, but deep down Ghost knew that she must. After all, it was his fault. He was the one who'd tried to leap the Maw when he knew he had no chance. He was the reason Winter had gone down there in the first place.

The guilt gnawed at him even as he stripped the bark from the bamboo cane and teased out more of the fresh, crunchy insides. He glanced over the river to where Sunset was still sitting, letting the morning sun warm his black-and-white fur.

He is a panda, Ghost thought. *And so am I, he says. So how did I end up in the mountains? Who is my real mother? Where is she now? Where am I supposed to be?*

Perhaps this new place was where he belonged? It was very different from their home on the mountain—he wasn't really sure yet whether it was better. It was very brightly colored, with lush green moss and golden leaves and flowers that Ghost had never seen before. It was also very warm and very wet, which made sense, since the huge river rumbled through the middle of it.

As he watched the sparkling water, a long-necked bird with a bright red leaf-shaped crest landed in the shallows almost right beside him. Shiver's head turned and the bird's eyes went dark—Ghost could see the instinct to hunt crossing his littermate's face. But the bird stared right at Ghost for a moment, ruffled its feathers, and then took off again in a smooth motion.

Behind where it had been standing, Ghost caught a glimpse of something gleaming orange and white under the water, and peered over for a better look.

"Those are carp," Sunset volunteered. "They're fish."

"Don't they ever come up for air?" Ghost wondered, staring at the smooth-scaled creatures under the water.

"No, only to eat the insects that float on the surface," said Sunset.

Ghost glanced around, wondering what else his new friend could tell him about this place.

"And what's that?" he asked, pointing with his nose toward a gray-and-pink shape that leaped from branch to branch nearby.

"A macaque monkey," said Sunset. "And look downstream— can you see those horns?"

Ghost looked around and saw something at the edge of the

river: an animal even bigger than he was, a bit like some of the mountain goats that the leopards had hunted. It had shorter horns, and its hide was covered in long, bright golden fur.

"That's a takin," Sunset said.

"This place is crawling with prey creatures," said Ghost. "Where are all the hunters?"

"There are a few." Even from all the way across the river, Ghost thought he saw Sunset glance at Shiver. "But the Great Dragon watches over all of us: predator, prey, or panda."

"The Great Dragon?" Ghost looked around, half expecting to see the creature he was talking about.

"That's right. But you won't see the Dragon." Sunset got to his paws, and his voice deepened and became more sonorous, carrying across the water. "It is the forest, and the sky, and the river. It is all around us, watching over us, and only the Dragon Speaker can hear its voice."

Beside him, Ghost heard Shiver give a small, dissatisfied mew in the back of her throat. "What nonsense. He means the *Snow Cat*," she grumbled. "Right? That's who watches over us. Why does he think it's a . . . a whatever a dragon is?"

Ghost shot her a glare, hoping that Sunset hadn't heard his sister being rude.

"Who's the Dragon Speaker?" Ghost asked. Sunset gave a short bow, dipping his head humbly, and Ghost felt suddenly self-conscious. "Oh—it's you?"

That must mean his new friend was a very important panda! If he could really speak to this giant invisible creature . . .

Perhaps the Snow Cat guided me here after all.

Ghost wasn't sure what he should say to someone who could speak to a being that was even a little bit like the Snow Cat. He was still trying to think when the branches above his head rustled and a few strange yellow fruits dropped to the ground, missing his head by less than a claw-length. He jumped and looked up.

"Don't be afraid," called Sunset. "Those are just flying squirrels."

Flying squirrels? Ghost thought he knew what a squirrel was, and they didn't fly! At least in the mountains they didn't. He peered into the tree, but he didn't see any birds or flapping wings—just two small, furry creatures scampering along the branches. Then suddenly they leaped, throwing their paws out to the sides, and he saw that they had long flaps of fur that caught the air, letting them glide easily to the next branch.

"Sunset, Sunset," one of them squeaked as they flew. "Dragon Speaker, the river! The river!"

"What's the matter, my small friend?" Sunset answered.

"Upriver," the other squirrel cried. "The floodwater! It's going down at last!"

"*What?*" For a second, the panda's shock made his gentle voice sound harsh. He seemed to take a breath and gather his thoughts before speaking again. "What do you mean, friend? Is the water really receding?"

"Receding! Going down! Less water!" the squirrel chirruped, running up and down its branch.

"Go up to Egg Rocks and see, Your Speakerness," said the other. "The river path is back! Back enough for a big panda to cross, anyway."

Ghost didn't quite understand all this, so he looked to Sunset, to see the other panda's reaction. Sunset looked a little as if someone had struck him across the head with a rock, just for a moment. Then he bowed his head and looked up again with shining eyes.

"Thank you for telling me, my flying friends! Ghost, will you go upriver with me?"

"All right," Ghost said, getting to his paws. "But what's going on?"

"For a year, since the great flood, there has been no way to cross this river," Sunset explained. "But it sounds as if, perhaps, that time is finally over. Come with me upriver to Egg Rocks—just follow the bank; you will know the place when you see it. Then you can cross the river and join your fellow pandas!"

Ghost's heart began to beat faster in his chest. Would he really soon be among his own kind, for the first time in his whole life?

"I will!" he said, and Sunset nodded to him again and then climbed down from his rock, vanishing into the lush green forest on the south side of the river.

"Come on," Ghost said to Shiver. "Let's go and see what all the fuss is about!"

Shiver got to her paws, her tail twitching with excitement,

and the two of them set off. They followed the river, splashing through the shallows and across stony banks, occasionally clambering over mossy rocks and along the branches of half-submerged trees, as the river wound through the craggy landscape. Ghost was aware of other creatures moving through the trees too, birds and monkeys and a small red creature with a long stripy tail, all heading the same way.

Finally they came to a place where the bank was wide and very muddy, as if it had been underwater only a few hours ago. There was a sound of crashing water, and Ghost saw up ahead a small waterfall, where the level of the river dropped suddenly by about the height of a grown-up snow leopard. Beyond the fall, there was a flat, calm place in the river, and five gray oval rocks, each a little bigger than Ghost's head, that, sure enough, did look a bit like a scattered collection of huge eggs. They gleamed wet and green, as if they had been underwater too until just recently.

Animals of all kinds were gathered around the Egg Rocks on both sides of the river. There was a great hollering and hooting as the creatures looked at the calm water and at each other. Some of the smaller animals noticed Ghost and Shiver and sprang away fearfully, but others were too busy staring, testing the water and speculating about what it all meant.

"Has the Great Dragon finally forgiven us?" wondered a golden monkey with a squashed blue face.

"It's about time," said the red creature with the stripy tail, who had climbed up to sit on the tree branch beside her. "We still don't even know what went wrong!"

"Goldenhorn, is that you?"

"Yellowback! You're alive!"

Two takins had approached the rocks and were calling to each other across the water. The one on Sunset's side stepped forward and dipped his hoof into the stream. He seemed to steel himself, then put his head down and trotted determinedly out into the water. It splashed up to the middle of his legs, but no farther. Finally he reached the other side, and Ghost took a step back as Yellowback rushed forward to butt horns with his friend Goldenhorn.

"Shall we?" Ghost said, turning to Shiver.

"Let's go! I want to see what's on the other side!" Shiver mewed.

Gingerly Ghost stepped out into the water. It wasn't quite as cold as the streams of melting ice in the mountains, but he had never been up to his belly in rushing water before. The sensation of it churning over his paws made him feel unsteady. Shiver seemed to be a little more poised than him, as usual, but she was also smaller, and her lungs were still weaker than they should have been. He looked back, thinking he might offer to carry her on his back, but he saw the determined look on her face as she held her head up above the water, and stopped himself.

Together they made their way across the slippery stones, struggling to keep a paw hold against the ever-flowing water. Ghost tried to dig his claws in between the rocks, but found that it only unbalanced him more. One paw slid out from under him, and he heard the assembled animals gasp as he caught himself against one of the big oval rocks, his heart hammering. Suddenly he felt very aware of the waterfall, only a few bear-lengths away, and the much deeper river beyond....

"You can do it, Ghost!" called a voice. Ghost looked up and saw Sunset appearing at the far bank. The animals all parted respectfully to let him through. Ghost steeled himself and pushed off from the rock, careful where he was placing his paws. He fixed his gaze on the bank and didn't stop walking, slowly and steadily, until he felt his belly lift out of the water. He paused on the more solid ground for a moment and turned, watching with a glow of pride as Shiver pulled herself up to join him, gasping for breath, eyes bright with triumph.

As soon as Ghost looked toward Sunset and took in a deep breath of his own, his nostrils filled with the strong, tasty scent of bamboo. It was much more plentiful on this side of the river, and he sniffed a few times, his stomach rumbling.

"Welcome, friends," said Sunset, walking down to the edge of the river to greet them. As he approached, Ghost realized that he was much larger than he'd seemed when the river had been between them.

Is this how big pandas grow? he wondered. *Will I be this big in a few years' time?*

The Dragon Speaker made an imposing figure close up, and not just because of his size. There was a scar down his flank that looked as if it had never quite healed properly.

Then Sunset bowed his head to Ghost's, and gently touched their noses together. Ghost felt a rush of warmth behind his ears, and another memory of Winter rose in his mind—but this time there was no grief or guilt behind it. He remembered her tongue, rough but very gentle, as it cleaned the soft cub-fur of his face, in their safe den, far away from here.

For the first time since her death, the thought of her made him happy.

"The Great Dragon must have sent you to us," said Sunset. "Welcome home, young panda." He lowered his muzzle even further to touch his nose gently to Shiver's forehead too. His warm breath stirred the long fur around her ears. "And to you, too, my friend. Both of you, follow me."

He turned and walked away, and Ghost paused only to shake the river water off his fur before hurrying after him.

They didn't walk very far, climbing up a long sloping path that looked like it had been trodden into the undergrowth by many large paws over a long period of time. There was bamboo all around, growing from between cracks in the rock, and the scent that Ghost associated with Sunset grew stronger and stronger. Then, finally, they emerged into a clearing, where the land dipped to form a grassy hollow, open to the bright blue sky.

And there, waiting for them, were more of the large bear creatures. All of them had the same black markings around their eyes and ears and across their backs, and the same surprised and curious expression in their bright black eyes.

Ghost stepped forward, his heart in his throat. There were so many of them! A whole pack of pandas, just like him.

At last, he had found where he belonged.

CHAPTER THREE

RAIN KICKED OUT AT a rock in her path, and it skittered off down the mountainside in a satisfying shower of pebbles.

That rock's going the right way, she thought. *Down, toward the river, toward the Prosperhill and Sunset Deepwood. Where I should be going.*

She knew she shouldn't indulge herself with thoughts like that. She'd agreed to this, hadn't she? She could have said no. Instead . . .

She gazed ahead with a sigh. Leaf, Plum, and Dasher were making their way up the slope, walking close together as she trailed behind. Leaf and Dasher were making attentively slow progress as they fussed over the older panda, while Rain followed, feeling awkward and regretting everything.

She regretted letting Leaf persuade her that it was worth traveling to some distant mountain on the slim chance she might turn out to be the next Dragon Speaker. That was obviously nonsense—Leaf might be, but Rain? There was no way, and no way they could be sisters, either. If she really was someone else's daughter, a triplet, and her destiny entrusted to a tiger who lived in a cave, she was pretty sure Peony would have mentioned it.

She also regretted letting the little red panda persuade her to eat termites. There had been no bamboo for the last feast, or the one before, but she should have stuck to the dry roots that she'd found and not let him talk her into sticking her tongue under that rock. The insects had tasted sharp and bitter, and she thought she could still feel one wiggling between her teeth.

But, most of all, she regretted letting Sunset know she was onto his lies. She should have played along with his fake vision. Her inability to keep her mouth shut had almost cost Rain her life, and now she was stuck on the wrong side of the river, with these crazy pandas, and getting farther and farther away from her home and her revenge with every step. She should have been more careful. She certainly shouldn't have laughed at him.

Even if the look on his face had been really, really satisfying.

It was so *cold*. She guessed that was a silly thing to think, as her paws crunched on the frosty ground and her breath made clouds in front of her, but she couldn't help but resent the chill on her paw pads and the end of her nose. She could see the snowfields, rising and falling into the far distance.

We could freeze to death up there. And for what?

Up ahead, Dasher was hopping and clambering over a pile of rocks, then running back to Leaf and pointing out the quickest and safest route. Leaf looked back at Rain with an encouraging smile that set Rain's teeth on edge.

And all this on the word of a tiger. A predator! Why did Leaf trust him?

None of this made any sense.

Sure, she had probably had a vision of a dragon once. Twice, if she counted the time she had been drowning. And, yes, it had had three heads, despite her never having heard any stories about it appearing like that. But that didn't mean this story about triplet Dragon Speakers was true. Even if that had all really happened, why would the Dragon save her life in the river, only to send her to freeze to death in the mountains?

That was if she even made it to the snowfields. . . . She started climbing over the rock pile, trying to follow Dasher's route, but she found herself struggling. She didn't want to put her paws on the sheer edges, glittering dangerously with frost, but she knew that if she walked in Leaf's paw prints they would be half melted and even more slippery. She made it about halfway up the crumbling pile before a rock tilted under her weight and she lost her balance, falling onto her belly across the stones.

"Rain, are you all right?" called Plum, from up ahead.

Rain didn't answer, or look up. She kept her gaze fixed

on the rocks, her vision swimming with embarrassment and annoyance as she got back to her paws and forced herself to keep climbing. It was one thing for young, strong Leaf to be a better climber than her, but older, wounded Aunt Plum? That was almost unbearable.

Rain shook her head and tried again to look on the bright side of all this. Weird things had certainly been happening in the Bamboo Kingdom, and it wasn't as if she knew how to get back across the river anyway.

Perhaps she would find something on this journey that was worth knowing after all. Perhaps Leaf would make it to the Dragon's cave and become the new Speaker, and then they could both go back to the Prosperhill and drive Sunset out together. That would be good.

Either way, if there was anything to all this talk of triplets and destiny, they would soon find out.

She didn't dare tell Leaf about her vision in the waterfall, or much detail about what she'd seen in the river. She already knew what the cheerful young panda would say. *See, Rain? That means it's all real! You're a Dragon Speaker!*

The idea was absurd.

Finally Rain reached the top of the rocks and found herself looking up at a sheer cliff face with a much more forgiving slope of gravel and brown grass running alongside it. Leaf, Plum, and Dasher had all stopped at the top and were staring at the cliff face, where a dark crack formed the mouth of a cave.

"This is where the white monster attacked," Plum said quietly. She took a nervous step away from the cave. "Can you smell that?"

"I can smell a predator," Leaf whispered. "Do you think it's still in there?"

"The scent doesn't smell particularly fresh," Rain said. She padded lightly toward the cave, sniffing at the ground.

"Be careful, Rain!" Dasher gasped. Rain thought about ignoring him, then looked over her shoulder and gave him a short nod.

"I think it's gone," she said. "Whatever it was."

She was actually a little disappointed, as she stepped into the cave and found that, yes, it was empty. A white monster sounded just as unlikely as her being a Dragon Speaker. She sort of wished it had still been around so they could have seen it in the light of day and known it wasn't any kind of evil spirit, just a normal predator.

The smell was real enough, and so was the tuft of white fur she found at the back of the cave, where something might have curled up to sleep.

Mischief seized her. She waited inside the cave for a few moments longer than she needed to, keeping as quiet as she could. Then she strolled out the entrance.

"Nothing there," she said.

The looks of intense relief on the faces of the others made her feel a little bad, but not very.

"My mother says there are leopards in the mountains,"

she offered. "Maybe it—*what*?"

She broke off with a gasp. The ground under her paws was *moving*, almost as if it had a life of its own. It trembled like a frightened cub. There was a sound like a colossal wounded animal roaring somewhere far away. Rocks skittered down the slopes, and a flock of small birds took off from a nearby pine tree, chirping anxiously. Dasher pressed his belly to the ground and put his stripy tail over his head, and Leaf and Plum huddled together. Something struck the back of Rain's head, and she spun around with a yelp to see a shower of pebbles falling from the top of the cliff face.

Then, almost as soon as it had begun, it was over. The earth settled.

"What was *that*?" Rain demanded.

"An earthquake," said Leaf, giving Plum a reassuring lick on the ear as they stepped apart. "They happen a lot up here. That was a small one, thank the Dragon."

"Small? The whole ground moved! What happens during a big one?" Rain asked.

She immediately realized that it was the wrong question to ask. Leaf looked sad, and Dasher shook his head.

"I've only been in a big one once," Leaf said. "We lost . . . everybody. All the Slenderwood pandas. All the red pandas. After we saw Shadowhunter in the Northern Forest, we decided to leave. We were all on our way to the Dragon Mountain. When the earthquake began, Dasher and I managed to hold on to the rocks, but the rest of them tried to run.

They were just . . . swept away."

"Oh," Rain said. "I'm sorry. Are they . . . all . . ." She couldn't bring herself to say *dead*, but Leaf clearly knew what she was trying to ask.

"I don't know," she said, hanging her head. "We didn't see any bodies, so . . ."

"They're alive," Dasher said fiercely. "They *have* to be."

Leaf nodded. "We have to believe it. And just keep going."

They began to head up the slope. Rain stayed closer to the others this time.

"The land must be unsettled," Plum said as they walked. "The kingdom hasn't been quite right since the flood. I'm sure this won't be the last earthquake that finds us on this journey."

"It's as if the mountain is telling us to hurry," said Leaf, her mood brightening a little. "We must find the Dragon before Sunset can do any more damage to the Prosperhill pandas."

She said this with a glance at Rain. Rain appreciated that her supposed sister wanted to make sure she was included, but she couldn't help remembering when Sunset had made up fake prophecies and talked about the wind changing and the seasons turning, and all the pandas had tied themselves in knots trying to work out what it all *meant*.

What if it didn't mean anything? Or, maybe worse, what if it meant the opposite of Leaf's theory—the mountain was telling them to turn back, that they were on the wrong path?

Still, she followed Leaf and Dasher for the rest of the day, stopping to observe each of the feasts, even though there was very little to eat on the mountain, and no bamboo at all. By the Feast of High Sun they had climbed to the top of the slope, over a rocky crag, and down the other side, and they were ascending a snowy slope where there was nothing at all to eat. They sat in silence for a few moments before walking on. As they trudged across a wide snowfield, they spotted a stand of trees and managed to find a few fallen berries, which they ate on the spot, though Plum said she wished they could carry them to their next feast instead. Rain tried not to roll her eyes.

Just after they'd stopped for the Feast of Long Light, Rain realized that she could no longer see the Dragon Mountain in the distance, and she stopped, her heart in her throat. What if they were lost? It ought to be just behind the tall rocky peak that rose in front of them, but what if it wasn't? She put on a burst of speed as the pandas picked their way through the snow and over the jagged rocks to circle the peak, but then she almost walked into the back of Leaf, who had turned a corner and stopped dead, looking at the path ahead.

"Wow," said Dasher, catching up to them and climbing up onto Leaf's back for a better look.

Rain gazed along with Leaf at the way they had to go. It was a smooth, snowy path along the bottom of a thin chasm, with rock walls rising on either side. And there, perfectly framed at the end of the path, was the Dragon Mountain. It was much closer now, its purple-tinged sides rising to a jagged peak. The bright Long Light sun caught the clouds that wrapped around it and turned them a deep, fiery orange.

Rain could almost believe that there really was a dragon sleeping there. The clouds could be its breath, and that dark, dark patch at the base of the peak could almost be the mouth of a cave . . . but if it was, the cave would be *huge*. . . .

"We're almost there!" Leaf breathed. She looked at Rain with eyes in which gleamed the same reflected fire as the clouds. "Come on!"

Despite her hunger, and the ache in her paws from walking on cold rock and snow all day, Rain felt a little of Leaf's energy rub off on her. The path through the crack between the rock walls was the easiest they had encountered on their journey, and the sight of the mountain in the bright sunlight gave her something to focus on. Soon they would be there, and they would know. . . . If the Dragon was real, it would give them an answer, a sign, something. And if not, she could put this whole Speaker thing behind her.

The path was cast in shadow at the bottom of the chasm, and the air was suddenly much colder than it had been. Ahead, the fiery clouds seemed to burn around the Dragon Mountain.

Then Rain's paws slipped as the ground shook again. The soft snow provided no claw holds and no way to steady herself, so she crouched down, as Dasher had done before, so that she wouldn't fall over. Leaf slipped back onto her haunches, and Plum staggered to the cliff wall and leaned against it.

But the trembling didn't stop this time. It went on and on, growing more and more intense. A loud rumble rose from somewhere nearby, though Rain couldn't see the source of the noise—it seemed to come from everywhere around her, like the sound of the river rushing over a waterfall. Then there was a sudden crack. Rain looked up, terror seizing her as she saw the sides of the chasm start to splinter and fall apart. Slabs of rock detached themselves from the walls as fractures snaked up through the ice and stone. One of them slammed down onto the path right ahead, sending a wave of snow crashing over the pandas.

"Get back!" Rain yelled. She grabbed Dasher's scruff in her jaws and scrambled to stand up. The snow was still trembling and slippery, but if she dug her paws in and ran, her momentum would carry her forward. She saw Plum push off from the wall and Leaf slip and slide to her paws, and then they were all running back the way they'd come, across the soft snow. Behind her, Rain heard another loud thump, and felt more snow hit the back of her neck. There was a rumbling sound of rocks crashing into each other, and then, very suddenly, the ground stilled and there was silence apart from the crunching of panda paws on snow.

She stumbled to a halt and dropped Dasher. She turned back.

Leaf and Plum were safe, but the path was no more. From

the sides of the chasm, rocks had fallen in and blocked their way, lying in a great unsteady-looking heap at least ten times as tall as a bear.

The mountain was hidden behind them, its light snuffed out.

CHAPTER FOUR

Leaf didn't understand.

As soon as she'd rounded that peak and seen the Dragon Mountain ahead, wreathed in bright clouds, with the smooth snowy path leading right to it, she had known what to do. She'd felt a kind of peace, as if a weight had been lifted from her back. All her doubts had fled from her heart, like shadows at High Sun.

She knew what she had to do. She had to go to that mountain.

But then . . .

Leaf sighed, and put out a paw to touch one of the huge slabs of rock that had fallen across the path.

It didn't make any sense. Why would the Dragon call to her like this, send Shadowhunter to tell her to come here, and then do this? Could it *just* have been an earthquake, and not some kind of message at all?

"Come on," Rain said for the third time. Leaf could tell she was trying to be gentle, but annoyance was creeping into her voice now. "We can't stay here; it'll be dark before long."

Leaf turned to look at Aunt Plum, who was standing very still a few bear-lengths away, staring up at the rockfall as if she was expecting another any moment. She didn't speak up to agree with Rain, but she didn't disagree, either.

Dasher joined Leaf at the wall of rocks, and looked up at her.

"We can go another way," he said. "We can find a way up to the top of this and walk over it, or go around it. There are loads of ways; I know we'll find one."

"But this is the way," Leaf whispered, mostly to herself. She was still so certain of it, but now the High Sun brightness of her certainty was starting to burn out inside her.

"It can't be," Rain said. Leaf turned to look back at her sister. "I'm sorry. I came this far, because I thought you knew where we were going, but I'm not going to wander the mountain trying to get somewhere I'm clearly not supposed to go."

"What do you mean?" Leaf asked.

Rain let out a laugh and shook her head. "I mean *that*, Leaf!" She jerked her nose toward the fallen rocks. "You know, the giant wall that could have crushed us? Look, *if* you're right, and there are really signs and the Dragon is trying to talk to us and the mountain has an opinion about where we're going, then this is the clearest sign we've had yet. If all that's true, someone clearly doesn't want us going this way. So I'm going home. I hope you find whatever it is you're looking for."

"Rain, wait," Plum said gently, but Rain ignored her and started to pad through the snow, back the way they had come.

Leaf's heart began to race. She couldn't let Rain just walk away. This couldn't be the end of their journey. She had to do something.

She turned and looked up at the rock wall, and swallowed.

"Wait. It's—it's just climbing! I can get over this!"

She looked back and saw that Rain had hesitated.

"No you can't," she said. "It's far too dangerous."

"Leaf's the best climber in the whole Northern Forest," said Dasher, with wounded pride in his voice. Leaf smiled at him.

"Thanks, Dash. I might not be the *best* climber, but I know I can do this. I *have* to at least try, Rain. I don't know why this happened—maybe the Great Dragon is testing us, or maybe it's just an earthquake and it doesn't mean anything at all! But I have to get to that mountain."

She put her paws up on the stones and started to push against them, seeing where there was give and where they were settled enough to take her weight. The first two places she tried shifted under the pressure, and a few smaller stones were dislodged and bounced down from above, narrowly missing Leaf's head. But the third was solid, and she climbed up onto it and looked back at the others again.

Rain frowned and turned to Aunt Plum. "Are you going to let her do this?"

Plum looked uncertain for a moment, but then gave Leaf a solemn nod. "Be careful, my dear."

"It's just climbing," Leaf said, smiling down at her sister before turning back to the rocks again. "Don't worry so much. It's just like climbing the Grandfather Gingko."

It wasn't like that at all. Leaf soon learned that there were no solid paw holds here. Even after she moved her weight onto one rock, when she moved off again it might slip or tilt and the whole pile might shift underneath her. She tried to ignore the small gasps of Rain, Plum, and Dasher behind her whenever a stone moved. She couldn't let herself startle or flail—she could start a rockslide that could crush them all.

She climbed, one bear-length, then two, then four. She reached up for a boulder that jutted out from the rest and gently put her weight on it. It moved a little, but seemed to stay put. She pulled hard, tucking her back paw into a crevice between two lower rocks to push herself up. The boulder stayed still.

But when she shifted her weight to reach for the next flat surface, something moved. She wasn't even sure what had happened, but suddenly there was a crushing weight on her back paw and then she felt one of her claws snap. She gave out a yell of pain and let go, slipping back and catching herself on a lower stone, which shuddered horribly. She hunkered down against the wall, trying to keep her weight from toppling her over backward. She managed to slide her back paw out of the crevice, and saw that her middle claw had been splintered right down the middle. For a moment she was afraid the shuddering rock might roll right out of the pile, throw her down into the snow . . .

But the rock stilled.

"Please stop," she heard Rain say quietly. "Please just come back down." Her voice was muffled. Leaf wondered if she was covering her muzzle with her paws, but she didn't dare turn to look.

She stood, and then got up onto her back legs and reached for the rock again. This time she picked a safer foothold, and managed to climb another bear's height up the wall of stones.

Her legs were starting to ache from constantly adjusting her weight, far more than they would have if she'd been climbing a tree or a solid rock wall. She looked at the stones near her and tested a few with a gentle push. One of them was covered in ice. Another had broken as it fell, so its surface was jagged and sharp. But the third she tried seemed solid, and took her weight as she leaned on it.

It was only as she was reaching for the next paw hold that she felt the rock underneath her jolt, in a new and horrible way. She looked down just in time to see fractures spidering across its surface, and then it shattered under her paw. She was falling. She grabbed out wildly.

"Left!" she heard Dasher yell from below. She threw out her left paw and it caught. Pain jolted up her leg as the jagged surface pressed into her pads, but she held on tight and braced herself as the shards of rock tumbled down and down. She had come so far. If she fell now . . .

"You can reach that black one, up above you!" Dasher called. Leaf looked up and saw that he was right: There was a big black stone just close enough to grab on to. She reached for it, tested it, and then pulled herself up. It was solid. She felt safe enough to turn and look down at the others.

They were far below her now, their worried faces just blobs against the white snow. She was close to the top of the pile. She was going to make it.

But what will you do when you get there? The others can't make this climb, especially not Plum. Will you push this wall down all by yourself, one stone at a time?

Well, perhaps she would. She steeled herself for the hard work as she pulled herself up the last few teetering rocks.

If I'm meant to get to the mountain, then I will, even if I have to move a small mountain of my own. . . .

Finally she reached the top of the pile. Up here, the rocks shifted beneath her with every shuddering breath. She gingerly put her front paws on the very top boulder and pulled herself up to peer over it.

The Dragon Mountain was still there, at the end of the

path, but the sun had gone behind a cloud now, and unlike the fiery light, the clouds seemed dark and ominous. The feeling of certainty was gone. She thought she could make out the mouth of the cave, impossibly wide and black.

"You did it!" Dasher cried.

"Well done, Leaf!" shouted Plum. Leaf looked down and risked giving them a wave with her paw. They waved back.

Rain was looking up at her silently, eyes wide. She cleaned her ear nervously with one paw and didn't say anything.

Leaf leaned carefully against a big, solid boulder and tried to catch her breath. The ache in her legs seemed worse now that she had stopped climbing. She looked again at the Dragon Mountain, and saw . . .

Something was different. Had the cave mouth *moved*? No, it wasn't the cave. Was it the clouds? There was something dark moving near the mountain, and from this distance, if she could see it clearly, it must be huge. . . .

Leaf's breath caught as she remembered what she'd seen on the slope when the pandas and red pandas had been lost: the shadow of a dragon, a black shape that was both formless and scaly, that moved past her in a moment and left a trail through the pine needles.

Could she be looking at the Dragon right now?

The thing peeled away from the mountain and seemed to spring into the air. It was coming toward the pandas. Leaf saw an undulating body, twisting like a swimming snake. The shape seemed to shift, so one minute she would see legs, and the next they would be gone, and then she would make out a long head fringed with wild fur, and then it just looked like a cloud once more. Her heart began to beat even faster, so she could feel the blood thumping in her ears. It had to be a sign! The Dragon was telling her something—but what?

"What is it, Leaf? What are you looking at?" she heard Rain call. Leaf couldn't answer—she wasn't sure what it was. It moved too purposefully and too fast to be a cloud, but surely too chaotically to be the Great Dragon itself . . . and there was a *sound* coming from it, like the noise of hundreds and hundreds of squeaking, high-pitched voices. . . .

"*Bats!*" she gasped.

They came closer and closer, sometimes forming the twirling, serpentine shape of a dragon and sometimes clustering into a thick cloud. Leaf realized, too late, that they were heading right for her, not slowing or veering from their path but speeding up. She gripped the boulder in front of her. She couldn't get down. If they flew into her—

She just had time to hunker down, covering her ears with her paws, before the cloud of tiny bodies reached the rock wall. They swirled all around her, chattering in their piping voices, too fast and high for her to make out the words. She looked up, cringing as a tornado of bats passed over and around her, thousands of tiny wings beating the air until it thrummed. The rock underneath her wobbled, and she shut her eyes and pressed herself against the boulder.

All of a sudden, the bats stopped chattering. There was no

sound but the rustling of wings. And then Leaf heard a roar all around her, like the warning roar of an angry creature. For a second she thought it might be another earthquake, but the stones underneath her didn't shake.

The Dragon . . . the bats . . .

But the noise was so loud that she couldn't think straight.

The roar went on and on, and then stopped as abruptly as it had begun. Pale light flooded in as the cloud of bats suddenly dispersed. Leaf looked up, blinking, as they flew away from her, away from the mountain, piping and chattering once again.

"Wait," she gasped. "What should I do? Should I . . . follow you? Please . . ."

She stood, and stepped forward with one paw.

The rock underneath her tipped.

Leaf panicked. She tried to throw her weight back, to twist so she could dig her claws into the rocks, but it was too late. The rock slipped out from under her, and the whole pile shifted with a sickening crunch and rumble. Even as she fell, Leaf knew that the sound would echo in her mind for a long, long time.

The shock was worse than the pain, as she tumbled and twisted down the rocks. Stones struck her paws, her flank, her face. She felt fur yanked out of her tail and another claw snapping. She heard Rain, Plum, and Dasher all screaming her name as she rolled, fell through the air, and slammed into the freezing snow at the bottom of the pile.

She didn't have time to even look up before the snow around her exploded from the impact of rocks and dirt, and then a boulder struck her side. The air was knocked out of her lungs, and the world went dark.

CHAPTER FIVE

"WHAT ABOUT DOWN HERE?" Shiver called. Ghost walked to the edge of the mossy rock and looked down to see her sniffing at a little hollow between two trees.

"That might do," Ghost said. He started to walk around and find his way down the mossy slope to her side, and almost treaded over a sleeping panda. The panda snuffled, turned over, and opened one eye to glare at him. "Oh . . . sorry," Ghost said.

The other panda huffed and put her paws over her eyes.

Ghost sighed, and tried to look where he was going even more carefully as he hurried to join Shiver. He didn't really understand the Prosperhill pandas' tendency to fall asleep at a moment's notice, especially after they'd just eaten. The weirdest thing about it was that their sleeping nests were out in the open, a few of them up in trees, some of them just in the grass or on top of the moss-covered rocks. If there was any kind of pattern to which panda had claimed which territory, Ghost couldn't figure it out.

"It's *sort* of sheltered," Shiver said uncertainly as Ghost found his way to her. She curled herself in against the side of the hollow and looked up at the tree canopy.

"It's . . . better than nothing," Ghost said.

"Not really a den, though, is it?" Shiver sighed. "Come on, let's keep looking. There must be a cave or something, somewhere on this silly wet mountain."

They walked in a widening circle around the clearing at the top of the hill where Sunset had introduced them to the Prosperhill pandas, sometimes following the well-trodden panda paths, other times striking out into the undergrowth looking for hidden spots where they might make a den. They climbed down and pushed through a curtain of vines, and found themselves near where a male panda was sitting beside a snoozing female, gently play-fighting with a small cub.

"Good Long Light, Ghost, Shiver," said the adult panda, a little stiffly. Ghost couldn't remember his name, but he managed to recall that the cub was called Maple.

"Good Long Light," he said. "Hello, Maple."

"Hello," said Maple. His eyes were wide and slightly fearful as he looked up at Ghost. "Why don't you have any black fur?"

"Maple," the adult male said quickly, "that's not very polite."

"It's all right," Ghost said. *I just wish I had an answer.* "I was born like this," he told the cub gently.

Maple's eyes widened even further and flickered to Shiver. "And is . . . is it . . . is it true you eat other pandas?" he said, all in a rush.

"No!" Ghost gasped loudly, and Maple flinched slightly. Ghost made himself step back and calm down. "No, not at all. Why . . . why would you think that?"

"You smell like predators," Maple whispered.

Ghost nodded. "We were predators. But we never ate pandas."

He said it confidently, because it was true. But he hoped the cub wouldn't ask him any more about it. When you needed to kill to survive, almost anything you could beat in a fight could be a meal. . . .

"I eat bamboo now, just like you," he added. "And Shiver would never attack a panda. She eats small birds and mice, that's all."

"But . . . but mice can talk," said Maple, horrified fascination growing in his face. "What happens when—"

The male panda hurriedly put a big paw on Maple's back and said, "I think that's enough questions." Ghost was a little relieved—the conversation was sniffing around the edge of distressing territory, and he didn't want to explain it to Maple any more than the other panda did. "We should let our new friends get going." The panda gave Ghost a hard stare, and Ghost understood that he was asking for Ghost to please take Shiver and go.

"See you for the next hunt," said Shiver, giving Maple a bright smile.

"You mean the next *feast*," Maple corrected her, wide-eyed. Shiver's ears twitched back in embarrassment.

"Yes. Obviously."

"See you then," said Ghost, and nudged Shiver into a walk. They gave each other a slightly awkward look as they headed down the panda path toward the river.

"Pandas really don't understand what it's like to be a hunter, do they?" Shiver said quietly. Ghost shook his head.

There were so many pandas here, it wasn't long before they came across another pair—two females sitting together by the path that led to the Egg Rocks, looking down toward the river.

"Have a little faith, Dawn," said one, who Ghost thought was called Horizon. "Speaker Sunset knows what he's doing, I'm sure."

"Oh, I'm sure the Speaker has his reasons," said Dawn. "But have you ever seen a white panda before? It's just a little bizarre, isn't it?"

Ghost froze. The pandas clearly hadn't heard them coming. He didn't want to stand here and listen to their conversation about him, but he also didn't want to make a sound that would make them look around and see him. . . .

"Do you think he lost his markings somehow? Who do you think his mother and father were?" Dawn went on.

"No pandas I've ever met, I'm sure. He said he was raised by leopards. *Leopards,*" said Horizon.

"And, speaking of leopards . . . it's all very well having that cub here, but what are we going to do when she's grown? Do you want a full-sized adult leopard living here?"

"I—I'm sure that Sunset has a plan. He's the Dragon Speaker for leopards, too, you know. Maybe he'll . . . teach her how to not be a predator, or something," Horizon said, but her voice was uncertain and uneasy.

Ghost glanced at Shiver. She was pulling a face of distaste, similar to the one she'd made when she'd eaten the bamboo.

His heart felt heavy as he quietly tugged her away from the two pandas, but he tried to ignore it. These pandas just needed a few days to get used to him and Shiver—he still fit in here better than he ever had on the mountain, and Shiver would show them she was their friend. It would be fine.

They headed back uphill and upriver, until Shiver stopped in her tracks. Ghost instinctively looked around for a cave and didn't see one.

"What about there?" Shiver trotted toward a large clump of bamboo, and Ghost saw that the thick green canes were growing in a circle around a hollow space. "Break down one or two of these, and we can curl up inside. It might be the best shelter we're going to find around here."

"Let's do it!" Ghost said, excited to have found territory he felt they could claim at last. He leaned over, just like Sunset had shown him, and snapped off two bamboo canes at the root. His mouth watered a little as he tasted the nice green insides—he would bring these to the feast clearing later. Then he and Shiver both squeezed inside the hollow space, and he sat down and leaned against the strong canes. They bent just a little, so he was reclining at a comfortable angle. Shiver sniffed all around the space and then turned around on the spot four or five times before curling up against his side.

"I like this," she said. "It's sheltered from the wind, and if nothing but a panda's jaws can break these things down, it'll be pretty safe."

They sat in peace for a while. Ghost enjoyed the distant sound of the river, and he was even starting to find the constant noises of birds and other creatures quite relaxing. Now that he had his own territory, he thought he could understand why these pandas spent so much time napping. It was actually very tempting to lie back and shut his eyes, just for a little while. . . .

A loud crack woke him up with a start, and he sat up fast and looked behind him, afraid the cane he was leaning on had broken. It was fine, but all around him the bamboo's leaves were wavering, even though there was no wind. Beside him, Shiver's ears were pinned back and she was sniffing the air.

"Panda! Someone's eating our den!" she growled.

Ghost pushed out through the gap and immediately came nose to nose with a large female panda, her jaws full of bamboo. She gave him a look of annoyance. Ghost remembered that her name was Blossom, and he noted that the two canes he'd left outside, meaning to take them to the feast, had been moved and stacked a few bear-lengths away.

That's . . . fine. I did just leave them there. She must not have known we were here.

"Um, hey," he said. "You probably didn't realize, but Shiver and I have made our den in here, so it's our territory now. Can you go somewhere else next time?"

"Don't tell me where to get my feast," Blossom snarled. Ghost's heart sank. "You should respect your elders! And, yes, I scented you in there. Strange place to sleep, but then I suppose nobody ever taught you how to act like a real panda."

For a moment Ghost just stared at her. He could see three other clumps of bamboo on this hill without even moving his head! Why wouldn't she just go there, when he'd asked her nicely?

Sure enough, Blossom bent her head toward the bamboo again. She was going to take another bite out of the den! Ghost couldn't just stand by and let her do this.

What would Winter do?

He took a deep breath, and then let it out as a loud growl.

"I said, this is my territory!"

Blossom just smirked at him, and then closed her teeth around the bamboo cane.

He couldn't let this happen. Ghost pulled his paw back and smacked it into Blossom's jaw, knocking her away from the bamboo. He was careful only to hit her with the flat of his pads, but Blossom reeled back and yelled as if he had drawn blood.

"What do you think you're doing?" she roared.

Ghost took half a step back, but then forced himself to stop. He faced Blossom, even though he was suddenly fully aware of how much larger she was, how sharp her teeth were.

"I told you," he said, clenching his jaw. "This is my territory now, and there's lots more bamboo, right behind you!"

Blossom was clearly not going to stop making a fuss. But instead of attacking, she sat back on her haunches and howled, "You clawed me! You beast!"

"I didn't—I barely smacked you!" Ghost growled back.

"What is going on here?"

Ghost looked up to see several more pandas approaching, some from the rocks above and some along the path from the river. Many of them were dragging large bamboo canes behind them. The two cubs, Frog and Fir, were awkwardly trying to move one between them, but they dropped it and stared at him, mouths open.

He turned to face them.

"I claimed this bamboo as my territory," he said. "It's only small, and there's lots of other bamboo here, but she wouldn't stop."

One of the other female pandas stepped forward. It was the one called Peony.

"Ghost," she said, in a voice that sounded strangely tired, "We don't have territories like that here. You shouldn't have struck Blossom."

"I don't know how you treated the leopards on the mountain," said a large female called Yew, with a lot less patience.

"But we won't have violence on the Prosperhill."

"It was bad," added Horizon—slowly, as if she thought maybe Ghost hadn't understood what the others had said. "Blossom's hurt. Do you see? We don't hurt pandas."

Ghost frowned. Why was she talking to him as if he were a tiny cub? All he'd been doing was protecting his territory! He glanced at Shiver, whose ears were pinned back in worry and anger.

"No one takes a leopard's territory," she growled under her breath. "You only did what Mother would have wanted."

Ghost saw Horizon and Yew exchange a glance.

"We won't have violence here," Yew said again. "If you can't keep to that . . ."

Then what? You'll drive me away? Ghost opened his mouth to protest, but before he could say anything, he heard the sound of heavy paws padding on stone, and looked up to see Sunset appear higher up the slope.

"Please, my dear pandas, you must have patience. We all must," he said, and looked right at Ghost. He climbed down from the rock, and even though Blossom looked up expectantly, he walked over to Ghost first. "You see, Ghost, before the flood, pandas could have large territories all to ourselves. But since the rising of the river, we have been living here together, and so we have given up any claim on territory, in order to avoid just this kind of argument. The whole Prosperhill and all its bamboo belong to every panda equally, from the Dragon Speaker to the youngest cub."

Ghost took a deep breath, trying to understand. "I guess . . . I can see why you would do that," he said.

"So you see, Blossom never expected you to defend your territory. Perhaps you should apologize for giving her a fright?"

I gave her *a fright?* Ghost thought. But he stepped forward and bowed his head. "Sorry, Blossom. I didn't understand about this place, but I do now."

Blossom huffed scornfully, but nodded. "I accept your apology."

"Then let us go to the clearing and enjoy the Feast of Sun Fall together!" Sunset proclaimed, and the pandas began to pick up their bamboo and move away.

"Sunset, can I ask a question?" said Shiver. The large panda turned to look down at her.

"Of course, my friend."

"Well, the river's going down again now. You can go anywhere you like. So . . . will the pandas spread out and find their own territories again?"

"One day," Sunset said. "I'm sure we will, but it's not time for that yet. There are still many dangers in the Bamboo Kingdom. For the moment, I have advised all the pandas that we must stick together, so that I can protect them."

Ghost nodded. He guessed he could see that striking out into the unknown wouldn't be right for every panda, especially not the younger ones who'd grown up in a big group. He had done it himself, and it had been a lonely and difficult journey.

But Shiver didn't seem quite so convinced. "Snow leopards would go right away, no matter what anyone said," she mewed.

Sunset nodded. "I'm sure that's true. And I would never force anyone to stay here if they didn't wish to—but I'm very glad both of you have decided to remain. I've seen that you are doing your best to adapt to life among the Prosperhill pandas, and I'm grateful. I'll see you for the feast?"

"Of course," said Ghost. Sunset nodded and strode away.

"Well, what do we do now?" Shiver said, sitting down and cleaning her paws. "We have a den, but that Blossom won't rest until she's eaten it all up."

"We'd better forget about it," said Ghost. He tried to give Shiver an encouraging smile. "Sunset's right—we should try harder to adapt. We've got a home and food. The least we can do is try to live like pandas."

Shiver just sighed.

"I know," Ghost said. "You're not a panda. But I'm not a leopard, remember?" He gazed after the large Dragon Speaker's retreating back. "In the mountains, Winter looked after me. Now we're here, and Sunset will look after you. It'll be worth it. I promise."

CHAPTER SIX

"LEAF!" RAIN GASPED. SHE put her shoulder against a heavy rock and shoved with all her might, her paws slipping in the snow. The rock made a screeching noise that echoed between the high cliffs as it shifted and fell. As soon as it was out of the way, Dasher sprang up beside her and started digging, throwing dust and snow and small rocks aside with his nimble paws.

"Please hurry," said Plum. Rain could hear the soft crunch of snow as she raked it with her claws.

Rain seized another rock between her paws and heaved it out of the way, and finally saw a flash of black fur, and then a white grip pad, and then the rest of Leaf's back paws.

"Leaf," she said again. "We're here, we've got you. . . ." *Don't be dead.* She couldn't bear to voice the thought aloud. She concentrated on moving the rocks, and finally she saw the fur on

Leaf's chest rising and falling with a shuddering breath. She pressed her muzzle into the dust, gripped the fur on Leaf's back like a mother panda grabbing hold of her cub, and pulled. For a moment she thought Leaf might still be trapped, and she might even be hurting her, but then they both slid backward.

"Keep pulling!" Plum gasped, and Rain focused all her strength on scooting back, dragging Leaf with her, as stones tumbled into the space she had left, sending up sprays of freezing snow and dust. For a moment, even when she was sure they were a safe distance from the rock wall, Rain kept her grip on Leaf's fur, just in case. Then the crash of stones stopped, and she let go and started to lick Leaf's face.

Plum hurried over, and Dasher lay down in the snow with his small face near the top of Leaf's head.

"Leaf, are you all right? Please, speak to me," Dasher mewled.

Leaf let out a long groan, and opened her eyes. "Oh, *Dragon*," she moaned. "Ow."

"Can you stand?" Rain asked. She could feel the air growing even colder as the sun sank toward the horizon. There was no shelter here, and the earth could quake at any moment. If they were stuck here with Leaf until she could walk again . . . If Leaf *couldn't* walk again . . .

Stiffly, and with a lot of wincing, Leaf managed to sit up, and then staggered to her paws.

"Everything hurts," Leaf said faintly, "but I think I'm all right. A couple of scratches and broken claws. Nothing worse."

"Thank the Dragon," Plum said, nuzzling against Leaf's cheek.

Rain pressed her own forehead to Leaf's. Even if they weren't sisters, she was glad the other panda was all right. Then she stepped back, letting Plum and Dasher cuddle up to Leaf as she got her breath back.

She let them all recover for as long as she could bear to. "We need to go," she said at last. "It's Sun Fall. We should find shelter before Moon Climb. We can start to head back down the mountain tomorrow."

"I'm not going back, not to where we came from," said Leaf.

Rain threw her head back, completely exasperated. "Are you *serious*, Leaf? You still think we're destined to go to that mountain? Even if the Great Dragon is real, don't you think it's told you pretty clearly how it feels? It threw a pile of rocks in your path, and when you wouldn't take that for an answer, it chucked you off the top and almost crushed you! I don't know if I believe in signs and visions, but even I think there's *no way* to see that as a welcome. Just face it—we got our answer. We're not Dragon Speakers!"

Leaf sat and listened to Rain in silence, and Rain felt a little bad as she came to the end of her rant and Leaf was still quiet, swaying very slightly, with a trickle of blood seeping through the fur on her cheek.

"You're right about some of it," Leaf said. "We're not meant to be here. Not *yet*. I think I know what happened. The Dragon *was* trying to warn me: it's not the right *time*. We're triplets. So where's the third one? We need to go and find them, and bring them back here with us."

"Oh, is that all?" Rain snapped. "And I suppose all that came to you in a vision while you were falling? Maybe you did hit your head after all," she added. "You're going to have to accept it sometime. *All* of you. The tiger was lying to you. We're not sisters! And we're not special! But we *are* going to starve to death up here, if we don't freeze to death first."

"No!" Leaf shook her head vigorously, and then had to pause, swaying dizzily on the spot. Dasher hurried to her side and tried to prop her up. "It's the truth. I know it is! And you'd know it, too, if you'd stop being so stubborn and selfish."

Rain blew out an angry breath in a thick cloud. "How dare—"

"Please, let's all stay calm," said Plum, stepping between Rain and Leaf. Rain glared at her, even angrier than before. She wasn't going to hurt Leaf! How could Plum imply that she would?

"The bats," Leaf said in a small voice. "Didn't you see them?"

Rain frowned. "Yes? They swarmed you, and then knocked you off the rocks. What about it?"

"I think they were trying to tell me something."

Rain rolled her eyes, but Leaf pressed on.

"I mean it. I heard the Dragon roaring while the bats surrounded me. And they formed the shape of a dragon in the air. Didn't you see it as they flew off?"

"I was a bit busy running to dig you out from under a pile of rocks," Rain said. She sighed. Whatever Leaf thought she had seen, they couldn't get distracted by it now. "Look, I'm sorry I snapped at you. We're not going to settle the future of the Bamboo Kingdom standing here in the open, though. And we won't do it if we freeze to death on the side of the mountain, either. Can we *please* find somewhere to shelter, and something to eat, and leave this for tomorrow?"

"*That* I agree with," said Dasher. He was shivering, kneading the snow under him with his paws.

"Of course," Leaf said. "Let's go."

The four of them began the long trudge back up and over the mountain peak. It was slow going, with Leaf and Plum both injured and all of them stiff with cold. Rain kept a sharp eye out for anything that could provide shelter or food, but she also noticed that Leaf and Dasher walked close together, their heads bent in low conversation. Occasionally Leaf looked up to check on Plum, or to give Rain a worried look.

It's true that I'm sorry for getting so angry, Rain thought. *But I'm not sorry for saying what I thought. . . .*

They finally found a sort of cave, really just a spot underneath a large overhang that was a little sheltered from the snow, and Dasher dug around until he found some roots and grubs that had made the place their home. Rain slumped down with her back against the rock and chewed on a root. It tasted bitter, but it was food.

"Great Dragon, at the Feast of Moon Climb your humble

pandas bow before you," intoned Plum. Rain paused in her chewing, feeling embarrassed that she hadn't thought to wait. "Thank you for the gift of these roots, and the bravery you bestow upon us."

The others tucked into their meager Moon Climb feast, Leaf looking especially thoughtful as she chewed.

Rain gazed out at the mountain as she ate. She had never seen the Bamboo Kingdom from a vantage point like this: white mountain peaks rising and falling to their left, snow gleaming under the moon, while ahead and to the right the hill dropped away and there were scattered clumps of pine trees, then more and more green as the peaks softened into the hills and valleys of the Northern Forest. Somewhere, lost in the darkness, the river was rushing through the kingdom, and the Prosperhill pandas were sitting down for their Moon Climb feast.

Is Mother all right? Is Pebble? They don't know what I know, but Sunset doesn't know that. What if he's hurt them?

"Rain?" Leaf said. "I think we need to talk about what happens next."

Rain sighed, and turned to look at Leaf. "What do you think happens next?" she asked.

She sort of knew, from the way Leaf looked at Dasher, that she wasn't going to like the answer very much.

"I've been thinking. I'm sure I need to follow the bats. I saw the sign they were giving me, and the direction they went. I believe I can find them, if I set off tonight."

Rain wasn't exactly shocked, but she stared at Leaf with exhausted horror.

She really is that crazy. She's desperate to find meaning in all this, and she'll cling on to anything she can convince herself is a sign.

What could Rain say to stop her? Climbing the mountain had been bad enough, but at least the Dragon Mountain stood still. Was Leaf really going to drag them all off chasing bats?

One thing I do know: I absolutely won't be doing that. . . .

But before Rain could say so, Plum let out a heavy sigh.

"Leaf . . . I wish I could go with you," the older panda said. "But I don't think I can go any farther. I must return to the forest and find the others, if they're still alive. The white monster's claw marks ache in this cold. I'm sorry."

"I understand," Leaf said quickly. "Completely. I wish we could stay together, but I don't want you to hurt yourself. Dasher and I will go."

She turned to look at Rain.

"And you're welcome to join us, if you want."

Warmth filled Rain's heart. Leaf was trying so hard.

"I can't," she said. "I have to get back to the Southern Forest somehow. I need to expose Sunset for the fraud he is."

"No, Rain. It's too dangerous," Plum said. "He almost killed you once! I won't let you go back alone. You're my niece, and it's my duty to protect you. If you won't go with Leaf, why not come with me to find the Slenderwood pandas?"

"That's a good idea," Leaf said. "They'll be able to help you."

"And we'll be able to find each other again," said Dasher.

They all looked expectantly at Rain. She felt their attention on her like a sunbeam piercing through clouds.

She sighed.

"All right," she said softly. "I'll go with Plum. You two had better get going, if you want to catch up with those bats."

"Right," said Dasher. He walked up to Rain and, slightly to her surprise, butted his head affectionately against her shoulder. "It was nice to meet you, Rain."

"You too," Rain murmured.

Leaf walked up to Plum and bowed her head for her aunt to nuzzle between her ears.

"Good luck," Plum said. "I truly couldn't be prouder."

Leaf looked up with watery eyes. "I hope you find the others. We'll be together again soon, I know it."

She and Dasher walked to the edge of the overhang, paused to look back for just a second, and were gone, climbing down the slope out of sight.

Chasing after bats, Rain thought, staring after them. It seemed crazy, but it was a kind of crazy Rain found she could respect. *Leaf knows exactly where she needs to be.*

And so do I.

Rain and Plum slept under the overhang, huddled together for warmth, and at Gray Light the next day they thanked the Dragon for the wisdom it bestowed on them and set out to make the journey down the mountain.

It was quicker than the climb up. To Rain's relief, Plum's injuries seemed to benefit from the warmer air. They had to take the safest, gentlest slopes, which added some time onto the journey, but with every step Rain's mood lightened. She was heading in the right direction at last. She also knew that every step brought them closer to where they might find some actual bamboo to feast on, and that thought kept her walking when her paws were aching and her nose was dry and crusty from the cold mountain air.

Whenever they stopped to catch their breath or have a meager, unsatisfying feast, Plum asked Rain questions. What was life like in the Prosperhill, before Sunset returned? How many pandas were there? Who led the blessings for the feasts? What did Rain like doing best? Did she have lots of friends there? What were Peony and Pebble like?

Rain answered her haltingly, trying to tell herself that they were just making conversation. She even asked Plum some questions. But she just couldn't help feeling awkward about it all—before every answer, she held back the same thought.

I am not your niece.

Rain felt painfully aware of the fact that Plum thought she was getting to know a long-lost member of her family, and she didn't know what to do about it. It would be rude, not to mention annoying, to keep on interrupting her to insist that they weren't related. But saying nothing felt wrong too.

"I like swimming," she said, when Plum asked her how she spent her days in the Southern Forest. "And hanging out with

Pebble. Playing with the cubs." *Pretending to be a Dragon Speaker,* she thought, but decided not to say.

"That sounds wonderful," said Plum. "I hope—oh!" Plum stopped walking abruptly. She sniffed the air, her eyes wide. "Can you smell that?"

Rain sniffed, looking around. They had rested overnight in a clump of pine trees, surrounded by swirling mist, and all day they had been walking downhill into greener and greener territory. Now they were on the edge of a real forest, with gingko trees and mossy rocks, trails made by small animals and birds, and more scents than Rain could easily count. . . .

But then she sniffed again, and realized she knew exactly which one Plum meant.

Bamboo!

Rain rushed forward, searching the undergrowth, until she almost ran face-first into a whole stand of tall, green bamboo. It seemed to shine in the light of High Sun coming through the golden gingko leaves.

"Plum!" she called back. "It's here!"

"Oh, thank the Dragon," said Plum, flopping down onto her belly on the soft moss nearby. "Be a dear and break us off a few canes, won't you?"

A few canes? I'm planning on eating this entire thing, Rain thought, but she started by clamping her jaws around two thick canes and twisting. The crack resounded through the forest and made Rain's mouth water. She passed both canes to Plum and broke off two more, leaving another six or seven for a second and third helping.

It was almost unbearable, but she waited for Plum to thank the Dragon before tucking in. The bamboo tasted fresher and more wonderful than anything she'd ever eaten, after days and days of cold, dry roots and tickly insects. They both munched in delighted silence for some time, getting through the first two canes and then two more before Plum let out an enormous yawn and rolled over onto her back.

"A wonderful feast," she murmured, a soft smile on her muzzle. "And now a nap, I think."

"Good idea," said Rain, settling her back against the trunk of a tree. "Plum? Do you think we're close to the Slenderwood now?"

"Oh yes," Plum yawned. "It's not far at all. The others may not be there, but we'll find them soon, I'm sure."

"Good," Rain said. "That's good."

She fell silent, looking up at the blue sky through the golden canopy, watching the flickering green and the brown shapes of birds as they hopped between the branches, listening to the gentle rustling of creatures passing by in the undergrowth. Finally, for the first time in days, she felt warm and full. Even her aching paws burned a little less as she patted the soft mossy ground underneath her.

It would be a lovely moment for a post-feast nap. But she had no plans to nap.

It didn't take very long before she heard Plum's breathing slow and change into soft, contented snoring.

Rain waited another few breaths, then stood up, shaking off the sleepy warmth.

You'll be all right, she thought, looking down at Plum. *You're a resourceful panda. I hope you find your real family soon. I hope you understand why I had to do this.*

Very quietly, Rain snuffled around until she found some leftover bamboo, and made a neat little pile beside Plum. She wasn't sure if it was an apology or a thank-you.

Then she walked away.

She didn't know exactly where she was going, but if she kept heading downhill, eventually she would have to find the river, and then she could find a way across it, and then . . .

Then I face Sunset.

The worry she'd felt on the mountain returned, squeezing her in its jaws. *What's happened to Mother? What about Pebble, and Maple? Has Sunset hurt them? They must think I'm dead. What about his plan, whatever it is, and what about his deal with Brawnshanks and the other monkeys?*

Anything could have happened. She picked up the pace, clambering over rocks and sliding down slopes that Plum would have had to go around.

I'm coming home. I just hope I'm not too late.

CHAPTER SEVEN

GHOST HELD AS STILL as he could, trying not to even breathe hard in case he rustled the grass in front of his nose. Beside him, Shiver crouched, every muscle in her small body tense.

Over her shoulder there was a flash of bright red and gold: a bird that Ghost had been told was called a pheasant, pecking in the undergrowth at the base of a tree trunk. Shiver took a quiet step forward, and then another, closing the distance between them, her whiskers twitching as she tasted the air. Ghost knew she was making sure they were still downwind of the creature—up on the mountains, the wind blew clear across the snowy slopes and changed direction only every so often, but here in the forest you could never tell when a gust would bounce off a rock or swirl around a tree and give your position away.

Shiver's back swayed from side to side as she prepared

to spring, judging the distance, shifting her balance . . . and then she leaped, silent and strong, and her large paws found the sides of the bird and bore it to the ground. It struggled and screeched, flapping its long wings in Shiver's face. She recoiled, but tried to keep her paws on the bird—and one of them slipped off.

"Ghost!" she yowled. Ghost burst from his hiding place, thudded across the grass to her side, and used his front paws to grip the bird tight. Then he bent and took the bird's neck in his teeth and bit down hard. The creature stopped moving immediately.

He licked his muzzle, tasting the bird's blood. It was strange—he still remembered when that taste had meant it was time to eat, when it had made his stomach rumble and his mouth water, but now he felt no particular draw to share Shiver's catch. He sat back on his haunches as Shiver looked up at him with her tail twitching happily.

"We're still a good team," she said.

"You did all the hard work," Ghost told her. "Your stalking's getting better and better, and your leaps are more accurate too. You'll be as good as Mother soon. . . ."

They both fell silent and still for a moment. The memory of Winter's fall crept up on Ghost again, but he tried to push it away and think of her hunting instead: the way she always outsmarted her prey, the power in her strides as she pounced.

Shiver's ears twitched, and she pawed at the ground. Then she looked up and smiled, blinking at Ghost. "Well, maybe not that good—but thank you."

She put a paw on her prey and shut her eyes.

"We thank the Snow Cat," she said, "for giving us this prey. May you leave your paw prints in the snow, that we may follow them."

Ghost bowed his head respectfully, but he couldn't help wondering if Shiver should have asked the Snow Cat to leave its prints in the mud instead. Could the Snow Cat even find them down here?

"Do you want some?" Shiver asked him. He shook his head. Shiver's tail twitched excitedly again. "All right. More for me!" she mewed, and bent her head to start biting into the pheasant.

"I'll see you later," Ghost said. He looked up at the sky, trying to find the position of the sun. "I think it might be feast time again—I'm going to go and see."

"Mm-hmm," Shiver said through a mouthful of brightly colored feathers. Ghost chuckled and turned to go. He sort of wished that Shiver could come to the feast with him, but he guessed that the other pandas wouldn't want to watch her eat her prey. And anyway, even though prey was plentiful and competitors were few here, Shiver would probably stick to the routine they'd learned in the mountains: guard your prey, and eat a little at a time over the course of days, to make it last as long as possible. It seemed like being a panda was the complete opposite—they ate as much as they could, but only at certain times. . . .

Sure enough, when he arrived in the feast clearing, he found it full of pandas happily munching on bamboo canes and chatting to each other. Sunset waved to him, and he waved back a little awkwardly. He had eaten some bamboo not long ago, by himself—was it okay to join a feast if you weren't that hungry? Maybe he should go away and try to be in time for the next one. . . .

"Hello, Ghost," said the female panda called Peony. "Why don't you join us?"

Ghost walked over and awkwardly sat down next to her. He liked her, but she was sitting with Blossom, who hadn't warmed up to him even a little since their clash over the bamboo den.

Peony pushed a cane toward Ghost, and he smiled nervously.

"I, um . . . I ate a little while ago," he said.

"At the Feast of High Sun?" Peony asked. "This is the Feast of Long Light; you can have some more."

"No . . . in between," Ghost said. "I'm still learning when the feasts are. I'm sorry," he added quickly. "In the mountains we had to eat whenever we had the chance."

"Sounds like a terrible way to live," said Blossom, rolling her eyes.

"Why don't you practice saying the blessing?" Peony urged. "You can just take a mouthful."

"All right," Ghost said. He picked a pawful of leaves from the cane. Eating them wouldn't exactly be a hardship; they still smelled so delicious. He held them in front of him, and began the blessing. "We thank the Snow Cat for giving us this—oh." He felt the fur on his neck prickle with embarrassment as he realized his mistake. The pandas all around were staring at him.

"Great Dragon," Peony prompted kindly.

"Great Dragon," Ghost repeated. He searched his memory for what came next, but his heart was beating fast and he couldn't seem to find the words.

"Humble pandas . . . ," whispered young Frog, climbing up beside him.

"Right! At the Feast of Long Light, your humble pandas bow before you. Thank you for the gift of the bamboo, and the . . . uh . . ." Oh, Snow Cat, what was the virtue for Long Light? Was it bravery? Maybe cleverness?

"Endurance," said Peony.

"The endurance you bestow upon us," Ghost said in a rush, and then stuffed the leaves into his mouth, just relieved to have made it to the end of the blessing at last.

Several of the assembled pandas nodded at him in satisfaction, but a few gave each other significant glances and shook their heads.

"What is this *Snow Cat?*" Blossom said. "Sounds like a rival to the Great Dragon to me. Did you mean to insult the Dragon, white cub?"

"Wha—No!" Ghost swallowed quickly. "No, not at all. It's just what Mother—what the leopards used to say."

Even as he said this, though, he felt a little stab of regret.

The Snow Cat is real. I saw its paw prints in the snow. I shouldn't pretend it's just something Winter invented. . . .

"Wait," Blossom said, peering closely at Ghost. "Is that *blood* on your muzzle?" She reeled back in dramatic disgust, and all the pandas turned to stare at Ghost again.

"It—it might be," Ghost said, though he knew for certain that it was. "I went hunting with Shiver. We caught a pheasant."

The looks of dismay on the pandas' faces made Ghost's stomach twist with anxiety.

"So casual about it," Blossom said, in a voice that sounded a bit as if she was going to be sick. "What will the rest of the Bamboo Kingdom think, if we have a panda walking around spattered with the blood of his fellow creatures?"

I'm not "spattered," Ghost thought. "I—I only helped Shiver, right at the end," he said. He looked up at a movement from across the clearing and saw that Sunset had stood up and was making his way over. Ghost panicked just a little bit. "She needs to hunt," he added. "I didn't actually eat any. I prefer bamboo now."

"So you say," Blossom said, shaking her head. "But your fur tells a different story!"

"What's this about, my friends?" Sunset asked as he came closer.

"Dragon Speaker, I don't want to cause trouble . . . ," said Blossom.

But you will, Ghost thought miserably.

"But the white cub doesn't seem interested in fitting in here. He kills creatures, disrespects the Great Dragon—and he has come to a feast with blood on his muzzle!"

Sunset listened calmly as she said this, then turned his steady gaze on Ghost. Ghost felt himself shrink back, but tried not to look away.

"I understand that Ghost's appearance may be jarring for some of you," Sunset said. "But I beg you to be more tolerant. Ghost has led a very different life from ours, and I'm sure he has much to teach us, as we have so much to share with him."

There was a muttering between the pandas, but to Ghost's relief, he also saw nodding and some of their expressions change from judgmental to thoughtful.

"Ghost, why don't you come and sit with me for a while?" Sunset said. "I'd like to speak to you."

Ghost nodded and got up to follow Sunset to the spot in the center of the clearing. He felt worried and excited at the same time—he was being given a great honor, but he might also be about to hear a harsher judgment than Sunset had wanted to give in front of the other pandas.

Sunset sat down and patted the grass beside him, and Ghost sat too.

"Might I give you some advice, young Ghost?" Sunset asked.

"Of course," said Ghost.

"You must be patient. I can see that the others still have a little way to go before they get used to you, and you to them. Don't be discouraged—but it might be wise for you not to go hunting with your littermate anymore."

Ghost nodded slowly. He felt guilt gnawing on him as he thought of how he would tell Shiver that he'd agreed to that, but Sunset was right. He needed to try to be more like a panda, at least for a little while.

He looked up at Sunset, and the guilt faded. It was such a good thing he had the wise Dragon Speaker for a friend. The least he could do to pay him back was to try to follow his advice.

The young male panda called Pebble approached them with two long bamboo canes clutched in his jaws. He presented them to Sunset, as Ghost had seen the pandas do before, as a mark of respect. But then, after casting a questioning look at Sunset and getting a nod back, he pushed one of them toward Ghost.

"I thought you might want to share," he said.

Ghost smiled at the other panda—he was still not very hungry, but being surrounded by all this delicious-smelling bamboo was making him think perhaps he could have a bit more. And it was very nice of Pebble to offer, in front of all the other pandas. Maybe he was showing them he wasn't scared or disgusted.

"Yes, please," said Ghost. Pebble sat down near him, and together they picked the leaves from the cane.

"I wanted to come and talk to you, because I, um . . . I heard that your mother died. Your leopard mother, I mean."

The bamboo in Ghost's mouth suddenly seemed to lose its taste. He chewed carefully for a moment longer, then nodded. "That's right."

"Well, lots of us lost family in the flood, but . . . I also lost my best friend, just a few days ago. So I just wanted to say, I understand."

"Oh. I'm sorry," Ghost said. He paused, a little awkwardly, but at the same time it was strangely good to look at Pebble and see some of the same dull pain looking back at him. *Now I'm wondering how his friend died—and I bet he's thinking the same about Winter.*

"What was your friend's name?" he asked.

"Rain," said Pebble. "She was Peony's daughter, about the same age as us."

Ghost cast a glance over at Peony. She had been one of the nicest to him, ever since he'd joined the Prosperhill pandas. Was her daughter's death part of why she'd been so accepting?

"My mother was called Winter," Ghost said. "She died saving my life."

"That must have been awful," Pebble said quietly. "The river took Rain. We all told her not to go too far out, that the currents were too dangerous. She never made that mistake before, but then . . ." He shook his head. "It was terrible. Speaker Sunset saw the whole thing. She was trying to find a way across to the other side, and she just . . . swam out too far and lost control. She always loved the river. It doesn't feel fair."

Ghost nodded, his heart aching for Pebble.

"Winter was a brilliant climber," he volunteered at last. "She could leap up to—up to the branch of that tree over there, or higher, in one bound. She was incredible. But she was trying to climb up the side of a crevasse, and the earth quaked, and the ice broke. . . ." He stopped and swallowed, the vision of Winter's fall flashing in front of his eyes again. "What I mean is . . . she was doing something she was good at. *Great* at. It wasn't her fault that this one time, something went wrong. You know?"

Pebble's eyes lit up a little as he looked at Ghost. "Yeah. That makes sense."

He picked up the bamboo cane and split it with a single bite, then passed one half over to Ghost. Ghost took it and they sat together in comfortable silence for a while, peeling the soft green insides and chewing on them.

Pebble and I have more in common than you might think to look at us, Ghost thought. *Maybe I can learn to be a better panda from him. Maybe we can be friends.*

Finally the feast seemed to come to a natural end, with pandas wandering away or lying down where they had been feasting for a Long Light nap. Ghost stood up and started to walk off, thinking he should go and find Shiver, and tell her what Sunset had advised him to do. But before he could leave, he found Sunset beside him once more.

"Will you come with me?" the Dragon Speaker asked. "I have a special task that I think you would be particularly well suited to help me with."

"Me?" Ghost stood up a little bit straighter and his ears pricked up. "I mean, yes, of course! How can I help?"

"Walk with me," said Sunset, and led the way out of the feast clearing and into the forest. Ghost followed him down the panda path for a little way, curling around the feast hill, and then off the path and into the undergrowth. Ghost didn't know the Prosperhill very well yet, but he was pretty sure they were heading away from the river, deeper into the green forest. Sometimes the trees opened up, and he found himself looking up toward a rising series of hills and crags, thickly forested and wreathed in mist. It was a lot like the shape of the Northern Forest, but where those hills had been sparse, these were lush.

At last they reached the top of a hill and Sunset paused. "We're here to meet the golden monkeys," he told Ghost.

Wow. Ghost felt a burst of pride and excitement. The Dragon Speaker wanted to introduce him to the other creatures of the forest! Maybe he was doing it so they could go back and tell Blossom, and the others, that they knew he wasn't a threat?

Except . . .

Ghost sat down heavily and licked at his paw. He'd almost forgotten—he *still* had some flecks of blood on his white muzzle!

"Wait, Ghost. Why are you doing that?" said Sunset. Ghost

froze, his paw half raised to try to clean the blood away.

"Um—I thought—the other pandas wouldn't like it if I made the monkeys think we might eat them," he said.

Sunset chuckled, low in his enormous chest.

"I think you should leave it as it is," he said. "This will be an opportunity for *us* to learn from *you*."

CHAPTER EIGHT

LEAF LEANED HER BACK against the mossy rock, and gazed over at the big fir tree that grew in the middle of the clearing below. It looked a bit like it had suddenly sprouted hundreds and hundreds of brown nuts. Except they weren't nuts—they were bats, roosting in every crevice and on the undersides of the branches, with their soft wings folded at their sides.

Leaf wondered what it must be like, to travel through the sky with a family so large you couldn't even count them all. She wasn't sure if there were as many pandas in the whole world as there were tiny bats sleeping in this one tree.

There was a faint squeaking still coming from the colony, even though most of the bats were resting for now. It had been going on ever since Leaf and Dasher had reached their roosting place, but Leaf wondered if now it was growing a little louder, as the sun sank toward the horizon and the shadows fell over the valleys of the Northern Forest. The bats would wake up at dusk and then, if today was like yesterday and the day before that, they would feed for a while before they took to the skies and moved on to another roost.

It hadn't been too hard to catch up to them, using the scent of their droppings and the sound of their squeaking, which had just made Leaf more certain that this was what she was supposed to be doing. It was as if they'd wanted to be found.

"Where do you think they're taking us?" Dasher asked, rubbing behind his little white ears with his front paws and looking up at the big fir tree.

"To find the third triplet, I hope," said Leaf. "But exactly *where* . . . no, I don't know."

She chewed on the bamboo cane she had found for her Feast of Dying Light. There had only been one, sticking up alone on the side of a hill, so she kept chewing on the woody stem even though she had already eaten all the tastiest parts. She'd need every bit of energy she could get.

"So far I think we've been heading downhill and down-river," Dasher said thoughtfully. "But there's no telling how much farther we'll have to follow them before we find this other panda. What do you think your other sibling's like?"

"This might sound . . . I don't know, ungrateful, maybe, but . . . I do hope they're easier to get along with than Rain," Leaf sighed.

"No arguments from me," scoffed Dasher. "She's the

stubbornest panda I've ever met! Are you *sure* she's your sister?"

"Don't you start on that too," Leaf chuckled. "*Yes*, I'm *sure*. But I know what you mean. It's a relief to not keep having the same argument over and over. I'm just glad she decided to go with Plum. If they can find the others, and they get to spend some time together without having to cope with climbing a mountain as well, maybe Plum will be able to convince her. . . ."

"Not sure about that," said Dasher. "But at least they'll be safer if they stick together."

Something whipped past Leaf's head, and she flinched and dropped the bamboo stalk. But then she remembered what it was, and forced herself to relax as another bat darted from the tree and into the darkness, and then another, and another.

"All right, let's be ready to move," Leaf said. Dasher nodded and stretched out his back, waving his bushy tail in the air.

They watched the bats hunt, knowing that when they had finished they would take off and it would be time to hurry after them. Leaf gazed at the glimpses of blurry movement she could make out. The bats' way of hunting was still wondrous to her, even after following them for several days. Despite moving at speeds she couldn't even dream of, dipping and soaring through the air catching insects she couldn't even see, the bats never flew into one another or into any of the nearby tree branches, or rocks, or pandas. She could hear them squeaking as they flew around the clearing and zipped overhead. She was sure that she caught a few words in the high-pitched noise: *follow, hurry.*

Suddenly, all at once, feeding time was over. The tree shed its load of brown nuts, but instead of thumping to the ground, they sprang into the darkening sky and streamed away from the tree.

"Let's go!" Dasher barked.

Leaf dropped the remainder of her bamboo, scrambled down from her rock, and headed after the bats.

At first they ran full speed, bounding over fallen branches and bursting through the undergrowth, tumbling down slopes and keeping the bats in their line of sight at all times, a dark cloud against the darkening sky. But, as tiny as they were, the bats flew faster than Leaf and Dasher could run, and soon they had to pause and catch their breath as the cloud receded and vanished ahead of them.

But it's okay, Leaf thought. She should have felt worried to see the creatures she was chasing disappear, but she wasn't— she knew they could follow the scent, and they would catch up with the bats at their next roost. After all, the Dragon had sent them this way, and she had faith that it wouldn't let them get lost.

They stopped for the next feast as soon as Leaf found another small handful of bamboo shoots, ate as well as they could, took a short nap, and then moved on, following the trail of the bats. They walked through the night, still traveling mostly downhill, into thicker and warmer forests. When they stopped for the Feast of Moon Fall, Dasher sat up straight next to Leaf, his round ears two twitching shadows against the dark sky.

"Do you hear that?" he said. "I think that's water."

Leaf listened, and sure enough, in the quiet of the night, she could hear the sound of running water. Was it the river? She couldn't be sure, and they couldn't afford to wander into the forest to find out.

The trail of the bats led them on, up and down hillsides in the Gray Light and then the Golden Light. They napped briefly, and when they awoke, the sun had risen higher and the forest was awake all around them, with the cries of birds and a distant chattering of monkeys.

"Where are we?" Dasher asked as they splashed across a small stream at the bottom of a long valley. "This certainly isn't the Slenderwood. It's wetter and greener, with more moss and fewer gingko trees."

"We must be downstream from there now . . . I think," Leaf said, but she wasn't at all certain where they were in relation to the land she had known as her home. The only thing she was really certain of now was that they would find the bats' new roost soon—it was almost Sun Climb, and they would have already picked a tall tree or a big cave to sleep in through the day, meaning Leaf and Dasher would start to catch up to them—they never seemed to get as far away as they could have. On a big rocky outcropping, another patch of concentrated droppings showed them exactly the direction they needed to go. Leaf thought that the bats wouldn't have made this much mess if they'd just been flying over—she was almost certain they had circled this hill before moving on. Had they been hunting, or waiting for Leaf to catch up?

But as they pressed on, Leaf started to worry. The trail was still easy to follow, but there was no sign of the bats' roost. High Sun became Long Light, and they stopped for another feast, for the first time coming across a clump of bamboo large enough to make Leaf's stomach stop rumbling. The land was becoming strangely marshy, though Leaf still couldn't see the river, or even hear it anymore. Long reeds grew up between the rocks. Tall cliffs still rose on either side of their path, then abruptly dropped away, not hills so much as columns of teetering rock that looked like they might collapse at any moment. Sun Fall came, and Leaf and Dasher debated not stopping to feast, because *surely* they must meet the bats soon. But Leaf was glad that they had, because it was past Moon Climb by the time they next caught a scent of their quarry.

"Leaf...," Dasher muttered as they trudged onward, climbing up a rocky slope and emerging into pale moonlight at the top of a hill. "Could we be going the wrong way? I know we're on the trail, but ... could it be the wrong trail, somehow?"

Leaf stopped on the top of the hill and looked all around her. She had been trying not to wonder the same thing. "I don't *think* so," she said. "But I don't know why we haven't found them yet. It's like they just didn't stop to sleep today. Why wouldn't they stop?"

"Speaking of sleep . . ." Dasher yawned hugely, his mouth widening and his small tongue curling in the air. "Naps are all very well, but if I don't get some proper sleep soon, I'm not going to be able to go on much longer."

"Agreed," said Leaf. Her heart was beating weakly but fast, and her vision didn't feel totally under her control: things had started to take on a strange flat look, as if the next hilltop were no farther away than the closest tree. "Let's get down the other side and then find somewhere to stop until dawn."

They walked slowly, Leaf placing her paws carefully in the dim light, until they reached a thick grove of gingko trees.

"We can climb up and sleep there," Dasher said.

Leaf let out an enormous yawn and nodded, then reared up to grab on to the lowest branch with her paws and slowly pull herself up the trunk, until she found a nice wide crook where she could flop down on her belly. Dasher clambered up beside her and curled himself up on top of her back. The small weight of him was comforting, and Leaf almost immediately felt her consciousness start to drift.

The next thing she knew, she was staring open-eyed into the dark, her heart hammering. She wasn't sure whether she had slept, or for how long, but she was wide awake now. The night seemed colder, and Dasher lay sprawled across her back with his tail curled around her neck and twitching at her nose.

Was that what had woken her?

No . . . There was something else. A noise. Something below them in the forest was making a sound like a low groan.

Leaf lay perfectly still, her pulse feeling fast in her throat, and listened to the sound. Could it be the growl of a predator? Everything Rain had said about Shadowhunter came back to her all at once, and Dasher's fears and doubts too. What if they were right, that it had all been a lie and a trap, that he had been waiting for them to wander off and lose themselves, and now he was here to finish them off . . . ?

But she told herself not to panic. It didn't sound like Shadowhunter at all! It was more like the moan of a large creature in pain. . . .

Leaf shifted, and Dasher grumbled and scrabbled not to lose his balance.

"Wha—?" he said. "We up?"

"Do you hear that?" Leaf asked.

There was a pause, silent but for the strange groan from below. Then Dasher spoke again, awake now and with a chill in his voice.

"What is that?"

"I don't know. I think I have to go and look," Leaf murmured.

"What? No! Don't go down there!" Dasher got off her back, but sat clinging to the trunk of the tree as she started moving to let herself down. "It could be anything!"

"I can't just lie here not knowing," Leaf said. She slid, back paws first, off the branch and down the trunk, and thudded onto her haunches in a pile of fallen leaves. She sniffed. There was a smell on the floor of the grove that felt familiar, but repulsive at the same time. What was going on here?

The sound was coming from a thick patch of ferns, which lay under the shadow of two trees, almost completely black despite the light of the moon and stars dancing in the canopy of the gingko trees. She approached, and as she did, she saw there was indeed a creature lying among the ferns, as big as Leaf or bigger. It rolled and groaned again. Leaf swallowed.

"Hello?" she whispered. "Is someone there?"

The groaning stopped for a moment. The shape rolled over again, and Leaf saw a black paw, then another, and then . . . a black-and-white face.

"*Leaf?* Leaf, is that—" The panda broke off to let out another plaintive groan. "Is that you?"

"*Gale!*"

Leaf stared as Gale Slenderwood pulled herself a few steps out of the ferns, then collapsed to the ground, moaning once more. Leaf hurried to her side and licked her face, though the repulsive smell that had masked Gale's familiar scent was stronger than ever.

"You're sick," Leaf murmured. "What happened to you?"

"I don't know," Gale sighed. "I came away to try to pick bamboo, but then the weakness took me. . . . I couldn't go any farther."

"What about the others? And the red pandas? Did you get separated?" Leaf asked.

Gale shook her head. She managed to pull herself to her paws again, and Leaf rushed to support her.

"We . . . we made it here, together," said Gale. Each word seemed to take almost all her effort to get out. "Slenderwoods, Climbing Fars, all of us. We found the Clearpool. It was . . . good. We missed you! But the sickness . . ."

"It's okay. You need rest. I'll help you get back, if you'll show me the way," Leaf said. She turned to call to Dasher, but saw that he was already on the ground just behind her, staring at Gale's crusted eyes and weak stance. He hurried to her other side, though if she fell there was nothing he could do, and together they began to walk Gale between the trees.

Leaf cast a last glance back at the gingko grove as they left it behind.

Have we lost the bats for good?

She couldn't think about that now. Her family was alive, and they needed her help.

CHAPTER NINE

SUNSET'S PLAN DIDN'T SEEM to be going particularly well.

Well, part of it was—the part that really mattered, Ghost supposed, shifting his weight on the flat rock outside the cave entrance where he was sitting. After all, the golden monkeys had agreed to take him with them to where they picked the bamboo. They'd led him to this strange cave, the entrance draped in thick vines and surrounded by a forest of odd, stripy bamboo canes. And now Ghost was supervising them while they broke some off and made them into weirdly neat piles to bring back to Sunset.

But it didn't really feel like he was supervising them. If anyone was being carefully watched here, it felt like it was *him*.

He could see now why Sunset had wanted him to leave the blood on his muzzle. He understood why Sunset might want these creatures to be intimidated by him, a panda who wasn't like the others. The problem was, it didn't seem to be working.

Brawnshanks, the leader of the monkeys, rolled a bamboo leaf between his toes, then stuck it behind his ear as he lounged in a patch of sunlight, watching his troop work.

Shouldn't he be helping? Ghost thought. *Sunset told me to keep them in line, and I'm way bigger than him. I should make sure they know that the blood on my muzzle isn't just for show!*

"How much longer?" he said to Brawnshanks, growling a little.

Brawnshanks sighed and rolled his eyes. "Does the Dragon Speaker want his bamboo or does he not?"

"I said, how much *longer?*" Ghost demanded again. "The Dragon Speaker is waiting!" This time he bared his teeth and tried to puff himself up, like a snow leopard would if they met another leopard on their territory.

The monkeys laughed at him.

"Ooh, sorry," one chittered, picking at her ear with her strange long fingers. "We didn't know His Highness was *waiting.*"

Ghost stared at them with a growing sense of anger. He didn't understand it. Each one of them was maybe a quarter of his size or less. He could end their lives with a single snap of his jaws if he chose to! The sneering, snub-nosed blue faces of these monkeys were making it hard to remember that he'd promised to embrace the peaceful lifestyle of the pandas. . . .

"Big, scary snow panda," sniggered another. He flung the

bamboo shoots he was holding onto the pile, scattering the neat stack. "Think you're tough, Fluffy?"

Ghost just snarled.

"Why don't you prove it?" the monkey said. He pointed a long finger toward the entrance to the cave. "Go in! Right to the back! It's pitch dark inside, and cold. Monkey cubs go in; sometimes they don't come out again."

"Yes!" the monkey next to him hopped on her back legs and clapped her hands together. "Go in, go in!"

Ghost stared at the entrance to the cave, its depths hidden behind the curtain of vines. A shudder flattened the fur on his back.

The last time he'd approached a cave like this, he'd been with Shiver in the mountains. Desperate for shelter, worn out and miserable, he had gone into the dark and found something there that bared its teeth and charged.

Except it hadn't been a monster, or a hostile leopard. He'd only realized when he made it to the river and met Sunset. It had been another panda.

She must have been trying to get out of the cave when she rushed at him. She probably didn't know what he was. He would have smelled like a predator. But he didn't know that at the time—he just saw something coming at him, and pulled back his claws. . . .

Where was that panda now? Had he killed her? Would he ever know?

"So? Going in? Or are you scared of the dark?" the monkey

pressed, hopping to the side of the cave and holding back the curtain of vines with one paw.

"Are *you*, Strongback?" one of the other monkeys said suddenly. She was a little younger than most of the rest, bouncing with all her weight on one of the bamboo canes to try to get it to snap. "Why don't *you* go in first?"

"Shut up, Nimbletail," said the monkey called Strongback.

"You shut up, Scaredy-back!" retorted Nimbletail. It wasn't a clever argument, but even so, Strongback seemed to lose his appetite for teasing. He dropped the vine curtain with a flourish and walked away.

The bamboo that Nimbletail was bouncing on cracked and splintered. She pulled it from its root and dragged it over to the pile. As she passed Ghost, she sniffed at him and looked into his face. Ghost felt like he was being carefully assessed, and frowned back at her—although it was better than being laughed at.

"Don't listen to him," she said simply, and moved on, dragging her bamboo with her.

Ghost watched her go, feeling puzzled, grateful, and frustrated all at once. He guessed she was right—he couldn't let the mocking monkeys get to him. He just had to do his job, make sure they returned to Sunset with the bamboo.

He sniffed at the pile. It smelled strange, not like the delicious bamboo nearer the river. He picked up a small shoot and brought it to his muzzle.

Something slapped it out of his paw. He looked up,

growling, and found himself staring into the face of Brawn-shanks.

"It's for the Dragon Speaker," said the monkey, with a grin that might have been pleasant if it had been a little farther from Ghost's nose. "Wouldn't want anyone chomping on the Dragon Speaker's special property, would we?"

Ghost met Brawnshanks's gaze. "Of course not," he said as mildly as he could, trying to mimic the monkey's casual tone, but his fur prickled with embarrassment and annoyance.

Brawnshanks grinned and patted Ghost on the head. Ghost wanted to snap his teeth at him, but kept perfectly still. Sunset hadn't told him to actually start a fight.

"That's enough," Brawnshanks called to the other monkeys. "Pick up that bamboo, and let's get back." He himself seized the single shoot that he'd knocked from Ghost's grasp, while Nimbletail, Strongback, and the others struggled with the bigger, heavier canes.

Ghost didn't offer to help, which was just as well—even with the bamboo, the monkeys moved faster than he did, and they set off with no further warning, leaping up into the trees or scampering across the forest floor. Ghost felt a chill in his paw pads as he sprang after them. Memories flashed across his mind: his littermates speeding across the snow, or leaping from rock to rock, their lithe and quick leopard bodies hopelessly outpacing his. The dreadful bitterness of being left behind, yet again.

"Hey!" he roared at the top of his lungs. The sound echoed

through the forest, and a flock of tiny brown birds took flight nearby. Several of the monkeys stopped, and one of them even fell out of the tree they'd just landed in. Brawnshanks looked back at him, head tilted to one side.

"Sunset said you weren't to leave my sight," Ghost growled. He took a few steps forward, not letting himself run, feigning confidence. "*You* follow *me*."

He heard a few of the monkeys snigger to themselves up in the branches, but they didn't immediately take off running at full speed, which he'd half thought they would. They looked to Brawnshanks.

Their leader gave an elaborate, mocking bow.

"Of course! We should always do as the Dragon Speaker suggests," he said.

The monkeys didn't exactly wait and follow Ghost. But they never vanished into the undergrowth, either. Ghost jogged behind them, watching them as closely as he could without tripping over rocks or bumping into trees. When he could, he kept an eye on Brawnshanks, which meant that several times he looked up to see the monkeys' leader hopping across a branch to whisper in another monkey's ear or gesture with his long, thin arms and tail.

They're playing along, he thought, *but somehow I don't think it's because they're afraid of me. . . .*

At last they crested the peak of a hill, and Ghost saw the feast clearing at the top of the next, with a few black-and-white pandas already visible lazing around its edges.

"Stop," he called to the monkeys. "The Dragon Speaker said to tell you to wait for him here."

The monkeys looked to Brawnshanks, and to Ghost's relief, their leader nodded. They settled in the branches of the trees, resting their bamboo nearby or dropping it casually to the floor. Ghost hurried off, relieved to get away from them. They would probably stay put, and if they didn't, Sunset couldn't blame him for it, could he?

It prickled under his fur as he ran, to think that Sunset obviously had an idea of what kind of panda Ghost was—tough and brave, and able to stand up to Brawnshanks and his cronies—and Ghost hadn't lived up to it. It was the same sensation he'd had a hundred times in the mountains, when Winter had told him he would be able to hunt and leap like his siblings soon.

They think I can do it, but I'm not so sure. . . .

But this is different, he told himself. *I couldn't learn how to be a leopard, but I can learn to stand up to Brawnshanks. I'll do better next time! I won't be taken by surprise.*

As he made his way down the slope and then back up toward the feast clearing, he found himself gaining on a group of pandas who were walking slowly, large bamboo canes dragging behind them. For a moment, he looked at the group and felt slightly panicky. He didn't know all these pandas, did he? Two of them were Ginseng and Granite, but there were two others he had no memory of meeting before. Was he just being forgetful? He'd tried to learn all the Prosperhill pandas' names, but it was an uphill struggle. Was he forgetting their faces now too?

"You'll find the Prosperhill a lovely place to live!" said Granite. "There's enough bamboo for everyone, no predators—and of course there's the Dragon Speaker."

"I can still hardly believe it," said one of the unfamiliar pandas. "The Dragon Speaker returned—and sent you out to look for *us* and bring us here! Isn't it incredible, Vine?"

"Oh yes," said the one he'd called Vine, looking around her with a slightly overwhelmed expression in her dark eyes. "Incredible."

Ghost's worry subsided. These were obviously new pandas, ones he hadn't met before. He knew that since they'd been able to cross the river—and even before that—Sunset had been sending pandas out into the kingdom, looking for those who'd been scattered by the flood.

Ghost slowed his pace, letting the group stay far enough ahead that he wouldn't need to introduce himself just yet. He followed them up the hill to the feast clearing, and when they arrived, he stood back and watched.

Sunset came forward first, a look of pure joy on his large, kind face. Vine saw him coming and let out a high gasp, then fell to her belly in front of him.

"Dragon Speaker! It's true, you live!" she said into her paws.

"Please," said Sunset, nudging her paws with his nose. "Rise. We are all so pleased to see you, and to welcome you to our territory."

Other pandas started to crowd forward, sniffing at Vine curiously. Vine got to her paws and nudged the male panda beside her.

"This is my mate, Goby," she said.

"Can it be? Little Goby?" said one of the Prosperhill pandas. It was Azalea. She hurried to the front of the crowd, looking at the male panda with shining eyes. "Barbel's cub?"

"That's right," said Goby.

"I remember you from before the flood! I thought you and Barbel must have been lost."

"No, we made it to safety," said Goby. "We split up to find our own territories afterward, because the bamboo was so scarce, and that's when I met Vine. I'm sure Mother will find her way here too one day." Azalea pressed her nose to Goby's cheek, and the rest of the pandas gathered around, greeting Goby and Vine with welcoming nuzzles and friendly words.

Ghost stood back, watching them.

There were good reasons it hadn't been quite like this for him. He'd been with Shiver, their arrival had been a surprise, and both of them had smelled like predators.

But still, he envied the easy acceptance of these two new pandas. . . .

"Ghost!" called Sunset. Ghost looked up and realized, with a flush of embarrassment, that Sunset had spotted him lurking at the edge of the clearing. "Come and meet the new members of our family."

Ghost pawed at his muzzle, hoping that he'd have wiped

off the last of the blood before Goby and Vine looked around. Ghost saw the now-familiar widening of their eyes as they caught sight of him and startled a little, although to Vine's credit she called out a hello.

"Hello," Ghost replied, and started forward. But even though he had summoned him over, Sunset broke from the group and intercepted him halfway across the clearing. Ghost remembered just in time that he still had a mission to finish.

"The monkeys did as you said," he told the Dragon Speaker. "They're waiting with the bamboo at the top of the next hill."

"Good job, Ghost!" Sunset beamed. Ghost thought about telling the Dragon Speaker his doubts—that the monkeys had barely tolerated his presence, listening to him only because it seemed to suit Brawnshanks—but he didn't get a chance. Sunset leaned closer and went on. "There's another task I would like your help with later, after the Feast of Dying Light. Will you walk with me then?"

"Of course," Ghost said.

"Thank you, my friend. I'm so glad to have a strong young panda like you in the Prosperhill—one who I can absolutely trust. You do remember what I said before, about these tasks?"

"Not to talk about them," Ghost murmured, lowering his voice just in case. "To anybody." *Unfortunately,* he added to himself. If he'd been able to talk to the others about what he was doing for the Dragon Speaker, about how Sunset valued him, maybe things would be a little easier. . . .

"That's right. It's very important. Now, come and say hello to our new friends."

"Speaker," Ghost said. "When you say *anyone*, does that include Shiver? She won't tell any of the pandas, if I—"

"*Yes*," Sunset interrupted firmly. "It absolutely includes Shiver."

Ghost knew that Sunset's instruction was going to be hard to follow, but when he was actually looking Shiver in the eye, it was even harder than he'd expected.

"Where were you this afternoon?" she asked him, as she emerged from the undergrowth while he was tearing down bamboo for the Feast of Moon Climb. "I couldn't find you anywhere. I was worried," she added, with a reproachful twitch of her ears.

"Sorry," Ghost said. He swallowed. How was he supposed to answer this question? "I was . . . doing something for the Dragon Speaker." Surely it couldn't do any harm for her to know that much?

"Huh. I thought so. Doing what?" Shiver asked, the end of her tail tapping on the rock where she sat.

"I can't say," Ghost muttered. "I want to, but it's . . ." He trailed off. Even telling her it was a secret felt like saying too much.

"Well . . . okay," said Shiver. "You don't have to tell me or anything; I just wondered. Anyway, I'm going hunting after the sun goes down—do you want to come?"

Ghost winced. "I can't. I have to bring this bamboo to the Moon Climb feast. And then, after that I said I'd do something else for Sunset. Also," he said, all in a rush, "I'm not sure I should be hunting anymore. I want to fit in here. Be a real panda. They think it's creepy if I come to their feasts smelling of predator."

"*Creepy,*" Shiver sniffed. Ghost winced again. He wanted to take it back—he hadn't meant *she* was creepy—but she went on before he could speak. "Fine. I guess you should do more panda stuff, if you're going to live here forever. I'll see you . . . around."

She jumped off her rock and headed back into the trees, her long tail swishing low to the ground behind her. Ghost wanted to call after her, but what would he say? He couldn't change his mind. The Dragon Speaker needed his help.

"I have a story to tell you, Ghost," said Sunset, as they made their way down the hill after the Feast of Moon Climb. His voice was quiet, but the forest was still, with only the snuffling of a few small animals and the footfalls of the two pandas to disturb the silence. Most of the pandas had retreated to their little nests on a nearby hillside.

Ghost had to tread carefully; the steep descent proved tricky at night, with patches of ground and the sides of trees picked out in bright silver moonlight and the rest of the forest in deep shadow. He focused on placing his paws and listening to Sunset's voice.

"This is a story I have told no other panda," he said, his low voice rumbling. "I see great potential in you, Ghost, and your upbringing gives you a perspective other pandas do not have. That's why I'm sharing it with you now.

"You see, I am thrilled to have found Goby and Vine . . . but they were not the pandas I was hoping to see today. My directive to bring home wandering pandas has a bigger purpose. You and I are traveling now to the river, where we will cross into the Northern Forest and spend this night searching for clues. Your experience as a hunter will help with this, I hope."

"Clues?" Ghost prompted. "What—what bigger purpose?" He thought for a second, pausing on the edge of a rock as he judged the distance to the ground. "Who are we looking for?"

"Triplets," said Sunset. "My purpose here—the reason I believe the Great Dragon led me back to the Prosperhill in the first place—is to find triplet panda cubs. You may not know this, because I believe leopards routinely have three or even four cubs in a litter, but for pandas, if two cubs are born, one will usually not survive. Three living triplets is unheard of. Until now."

Ghost nodded, trying to absorb this. "So . . . they're important, these cubs?"

"Very," said Sunset. "The fate of the whole Bamboo Kingdom rests upon whether I find them in time."

"In time? For what?" Ghost asked, as they emerged from the trees onto the riverbank. The light was brighter here, and the water glittered under the moonlight as it split and rippled around the Egg Rocks.

Sunset didn't answer Ghost's question, but froze just at the edge of the trees.

"What was that?" he hissed.

Ghost froze too, listening. He hadn't heard anything before. Now there was the gentle rushing of the river, the chirp of a distant bird, and . . .

Something rustled in the bushes.

Ghost looked to Sunset, who gave him a sharp nod. Ghost stepped forward. He sniffed. Was it just a prey creature . . . or was someone following them? He moved quietly, slowly, tracking just like Winter had taught him. He smelled panda, a recent trail that wasn't Sunset's scent. . . .

He tensed his muscles and sprang into the undergrowth. It wasn't a leopard leap, but it didn't need to be. He slammed his heavy paws down into the bush.

But there was nothing there. No lurking panda, and no quivering prey creature, either.

It must have been a panda scent left from earlier. He paused, listening hard for any more noise, but he could hear nothing. He pushed his nose into the closest clump of bamboo, making it creak as it bent aside, but there was nothing there either.

"Must have been a rabbit or something running away," he said, turning to Sunset. Sunset nodded.

"You did well," he murmured. "I'm glad I chose you to come with me. We must stay vigilant." He stepped forward, letting the river lap over his front paws, and staring across the path, past the Egg Rocks, to the far shore. "This will be the first time I've set foot on the other side of the river since the night before the flood," he said. "If the three cubs are hiding in the Northern Forest, they won't be hidden for long."

He raised a paw, but before he had taken another step forward, his whole body tensed and he crouched down, the white fur on his belly touching the surface of the water.

"What is it?" Ghost asked, looking around, listening for more rustling.

"*Quiet!*" Sunset snapped. His gaze was fixed on the opposite bank, his black eyes wide. With trembling paws, he backed out of the river and crouched beside a tree trunk. "Get down," he told Ghost, and Ghost obeyed, hunkering down in the undergrowth.

At first he couldn't even see what had made Sunset so nervous. Then something moved, turning a huge head, one ear twitching, a pair of glinting eyes casting out over the river.

It looked, for a moment, like a giant leopard. But it wasn't just bigger: Its strides were longer than Winter's, its haunches thicker, and instead of spots, it had stripes of black across its flank and face that blended perfectly with the harsh shadows of the forest. It turned and opened its jaws to taste the air, and Ghost caught a glimpse of fangs as long as his paw.

"Tiger," said Sunset. His voice was so low and hollow, his breath barely seemed to stir the air around them.

Slowly, careful not to disturb the undergrowth too much,

Ghost crouched down even further. He watched as the tiger stalked along the bank, still sniffing the air and the tree trunks on that side of the river.

Searching for something? Or just looking for prey?

Ghost had been in danger before, in the White Spine Mountains, but he was always big, and he had his claws that never retracted and his teeth that could bite harder than any leopard's. It had been a long time since he'd thought of himself as *prey*. But this creature was so large, he was sure even Sunset would struggle to survive if it came to a fight.

Still, it was only one creature, and it probably wasn't interested in fighting a panda. Ghost knew that predators would always rather not risk being injured, if they could help it. The tiger probably wouldn't chase them if they didn't go too near. They just had to wait long enough, and surely the tiger would move on, satisfied that there was nothing here worth its time.

Except . . . no, the tiger was turning around and stalking back along the bank! It stopped right at the other side of the Egg Rocks path, and Sunset cringed back as it peered over the river.

It can't have seen us, or caught our scent from there . . . not across the water . . . can it?

After what seemed like a long time staring into the darkness, the tiger turned away and went back to pacing along the bank. Ghost swallowed. His throat felt like he'd tried to eat nettles.

"We can still cross," he whispered. "If we time it just right—"

"*No!*" Sunset hissed. Ghost looked at him and saw for the first time that his fur was trembling a little as he breathed.

The Dragon Speaker is afraid! Ghost thought, and glanced back at the shadowy tiger, a new and horrible respect for the creature creeping into his bones.

"Another day," Sunset added. "No need to risk it today."

He waited for the tiger to turn its back, and then without another word he turned and vanished into the Southern Forest, leaving Ghost to scramble after him.

CHAPTER TEN

LEAF, DASHER, AND GALE arrived at the glade that Gale had called the Clearpool just as dawn was breaking through the canopy above them. The journey from the gingko trees had been achingly slow, with Gale stopping every few paw steps as spasms of pain racked her body. Leaf could hardly believe she had walked so far from the others in the first place—she thought Gale would never have made it back if it hadn't been for her and Dasher.

This cannot be against the will of the Dragon, she thought. *I know that the Dragon wouldn't want me to let Gale die, alone and in pain.*

She held on to that belief as if she was gripping it between her teeth, even though at the same time she knew that they had lost the trail of the bats, possibly forever. Where had they been leading? What price would she pay for failing to follow?

Whatever the price, it was worth it when she helped Gale step out from behind a bush and found herself looking down a smooth, grassy slope dotted with the black-and-white fur of her family. The Slenderwood pandas and red pandas sat in small groups on the slope or in the trees around them, looking at first as if they were all basking in the bright dawn sunshine. But the smell of the place and the lethargic way they looked up at Gale's weak call immediately told a different story. The pandas were alive, but every one of them was sick.

"Leaf," gasped Juniper, trying to sit up. "You're alive!"

A chorus of surprised groans ran up and down the slope as the pandas and red pandas all turned to look. A few of them managed to get unsteadily to their paws and start to hurry over. From above her head, Leaf heard a familiar red panda voice cry out.

"Leaf? Leaf? Is she here? Is Dasher with her? Dasher?" And a moment later Dasher's mother, Seeker Climbing Far, was hurrying down the trunk of a nearby tree, almost dropping into the bushes below in her hurry.

"Mother!" Dasher cried, and ran to greet her. They wrapped their long fluffy tails around each other, and a moment later they were almost mobbed by weak but happy Climbing Fars.

Leaf let Gale sink down into a patch of soft moss, and hurried to greet Juniper as he managed to lope up the hill toward her.

"We thought you must have died in the earthquake," he said. "We searched for you, and we hoped the Great Dragon

would send us another sign . . . but it didn't." He sagged, looking tired and sad. Leaf glanced over at Dasher and found him
looking back at her.

I think I know why no panda here got a sign, Leaf thought. *It was me
the Dragon spoke to when we were lost. Without me, they had no connection
to it.* She guessed she ought to tell them everything that had
happened, everything she'd learned about herself . . . but was
this the right time? They were all so sick.

"We searched for you, too," she said instead. "What happened to you?"

"When we couldn't find you, we just . . . we couldn't carry
on up that mountain. It was too hard. So we decided the only
thing to do was find somewhere safe, a new place to settle.
And we eventually came here." Juniper looked around at the
hillside, and Leaf could see the relief and pleasure in his eyes,
even though they were watering. "It's wonderful here! Soft
moss, tall trees, enough bamboo—more than the Slenderwood, at any rate—and the Clearpool, of course. We are the
Clearpool pandas now."

Leaf followed his pointing nose. At the bottom of the
slope, the land evened out to a lovely, sun-dappled clearing at
the edge of a pool of deep-looking water.

Leaf Clearpool, she thought. It had a nice sound. She wished
she could enjoy it, but all around her the smell of sickness and
the groaning of creatures in pain filled the air.

"What is it?" she asked Juniper. "How did this happen?"

Juniper swallowed and shook his head, which seemed to
make him slightly dizzy.

"We don't know. But it's bad. The red panda Healing Heart tried to help, but he couldn't figure out what bamboo would work—and he couldn't get to it anyway, because he got sick too. One of the Leaping Highs died last night. And Hyacinth . . ." He paused, catching his breath, and Leaf's stomach twisted. She looked around frantically and found her slumped in the shade of a tree just as Juniper went on. "She's so weak. I don't know how long she has left."

"Oh no," Leaf breathed. As she watched, Hyacinth's son, Cane, cuddled up to her, curling in close to her chest. His little body shuddered with every breath.

Leaf hurried over to them, though the closer she drew, the harder it seemed to be. Worry and grief pushed at her, but she forced herself to walk right up to them. Hyacinth's eyes were closed, and even more crusted than Gale's had been. She was breathing in a shallow rasp. Cane looked up at Leaf and his eyes glistened.

"Hello," she croaked, and gave Cane a gentle lick on the forehead. "Are you sick too, Cane?" she asked.

"I feel like someone's chewing on my tummy," Cane said miserably. "And Mummy's too tired to wake up."

Leaf gave him what she hoped was another comforting lick. Then she turned back to Juniper, who had slumped to the ground nearby, misery written clearly in the sagging folds of his face.

"Is it the bamboo?" she asked. "Did you eat something on the way here that tasted wrong, somehow? Who got sick first?"

"I don't know," Juniper murmured. "I think . . . Grass,

maybe?" His voice was growing quieter and quieter, his head lolling slightly to one side, his front paws splayed in the moss in front of him. Leaf realized that just talking to her had exhausted him.

"I'll go ask her," Leaf said, and turned to leave him to rest.

"Leaf," Juniper called, stopping her in her tracks. His words suddenly took on a haunted edge that chilled Leaf's blood. "You might want to think about leaving this place. While you still can."

"No!" Leaf said. She didn't have to consider it. "I can't leave you all like this."

"Your aunt Plum wouldn't want you to . . . to catch the sickness," Juniper sighed.

You mean she wouldn't want me to die. But I won't die. Nobody here is going to die! Leaf knew it wouldn't help to say it out loud, but she thought it as hard as she could, trying her best to believe it. *There must be something I can do.*

It was clear that Aunt Plum and Rain hadn't found their way here yet. There was no telling where they were, or how long it might take them to find the Clearpool, or whether something might have happened to them. . . .

I can't think like that, she told herself. *Something could have happened to them, yes. But unless the Dragon itself tells me, I can't possibly know. And something is happening to these pandas, here, now.*

She looked around for Dasher and saw him sitting beside a small, unmoving mound of red fur. It was Twitcher Leaping High. She walked solemnly over to join him, and sat down close enough that he could choose to lean against her, if he wanted. After a moment, Dasher let his head fall against Leaf's leg and his tail curl around her paw.

"Plum and Rain haven't found this place yet," she said.

"That's good, I guess. It means they probably haven't caught the sickness, right?" Dasher muttered.

Leaf nodded. She could only hope that he was right.

"So what do we do?" Dasher asked. He tipped his head back to look up at Leaf. "What will you do?"

"You mean . . . as a Dragon Speaker?" Leaf whispered. "I have no idea. I think it's my duty to help, but . . . but wasn't it my duty to follow the bats? That's what I thought—and perhaps this is the place they were leading us to all along. But if it isn't, and if we don't find their trail again soon, we will have lost them for good. But I can't leave," she added quickly, as Dasher gave her a shocked glare. "So I guess we'll have to find the third triplet another way. . . ."

"Leaf," said a voice, and Leaf startled and turned to see a group of red pandas approaching, including Wanderer Leaping High and Splasher Swimming Deep. It was Wanderer who had spoken. She looked a little dazed, but not as sick as Splasher, who was weaving as she walked. "You were the one who saw the Dragon's shadow, up on the mountain," said Wanderer. "You led us to a better place then. The other pandas say the Dragon hasn't shown itself to them—have *you* seen anything? We need its help, now more than ever!"

Leaf felt Dasher's eyes on her. This would be the time, if

she was going to come out with it, to tell them all what Shadowhunter had told her. . . .

But she hadn't seen another vision, not since she'd been sure the bats were leading her toward the other triplet, and she wasn't sure anymore that she'd been right about that. If she told them now, they'd expect her to be able to help. What if she couldn't?

"No," she said. "But . . . I can try."

She closed her eyes. She tried to picture the Dragon Mountain, purple on the horizon, with the billowing cloud like smoke circling its peak.

Please, Great Dragon, she thought. *Your humble servants need your help—your pandas and their friends the red pandas. They will die if we don't help them. Please . . .*

The smell of the sickness was all around her. She tried to remember the black shape that had swept through the pine needles and shown them the way, the dragon-like shape of the bats, the great roar she had heard when they surrounded her. Then she opened her eyes.

But she could see nothing different at the Clearpool, except that a few more pandas and red pandas had gathered to watch, a nervous hope in their eyes.

She waited, and waited some more.

But there was nothing.

She shook her head. "I'm sorry," she sighed.

"It's okay," said Wanderer, a little too quickly. Leaf thought she was probably just trying to hide her disappointment.

"There's no reason it should work the same way twice."

But there is. Or there's supposed to be. . . .

Leaf could almost hear what Rain would say if she was here right now. *How much more evidence do you need? You're not the Dragon Speaker. You were wrong all along.*

"I'm still sorry," Leaf whispered.

"Maybe we're just . . . looking in the wrong place?" Dasher suggested. "We can still help. We're not sick yet. Let's go see Runner Healing Heart—maybe he just needs someone strong to go and find the right kind of healing bamboo!"

But when Wanderer led them over to the elderly red panda, his words were not encouraging.

"Test the bamboo," he said, scratching at the graying hairs on his muzzle. "But the termites . . . the gingko . . . I ate from every tree, before I was too sick to stand, and unless it's a rot that can't be smelled or tasted, it isn't in the food."

"What about purple leaf?" Dasher asked. "It helps with injuries—should we try to find some, in case it helps with this, too?"

"If you can," said Runner, then broke off as a spasm racked his small body. Leaf cringed and Dasher rushed forward to support the healer's head under his shoulder as his back legs kicked out in pain, then went still again. "Whatever you do, it must be soon," said Runner.

"Is there anything you haven't checked?" Dasher sat down and scrunched his eyes shut. "If it's not the food . . . what about the water?"

Leaf turned and looked down the hill to the dappled glade, and the gleaming edge of the pool. "Could it be?"

"Even from here it looks so clear," Dasher said. But they padded down to the edge of the water anyway. There was a flattened gap in the reeds where the pandas and the red pandas had stood to drink. Dasher walked right up to the edge and batted at the surface of the water gingerly. The ripples spread across the pool, perfect circles radiating out from Dasher's paw.

Leaf stared into the water. It was obvious how the place had gotten its name—she could see down through the water to a carpet of wavering reeds that grew across the bottom of the pool. It looked inviting and pleasant, a place where cubs could play. It must be fed from some hidden stream from high in the mountains. . . .

Dasher put his muzzle down and took a long sniff. "I don't smell anything," he said. "I think it's okay. It's making me thirsty, though!" And he bent his head, sticking his tongue out to drink the water.

But as he did, Leaf saw that the bottom of the pool seemed to grow darker. Something black swirled up from below the reeds, obscuring her sight, filling the pool with darkness. In a moment, the clear pool was black from edge to edge. She stared down into it and saw her reflection looking back, its eyes wide . . . and then it wasn't her own face, but the skull of a panda, rising up out of the water, its jaws open in a horrible moan.

She seized Dasher by the scruff of his neck and dragged him away before he could touch his tongue to the surface. He landed on his back in the grass, his paws flailing.

"What?" Dasher yelped, as he righted himself. "What did you do that for?"

"You can't drink it! The water's *black*!" Leaf said, and looked back at the pool.

The water was perfectly clear. There was no black liquid, and no panda skull. . . .

"Did you have a vision?" Dasher gasped. Leaf took a long, restorative breath, the first one she felt like she'd taken since they had found the others.

"I think so! I saw a skull, as if the pool was . . . *dead* somehow. I think the Great Dragon has spoken to me. It wants me to know the sickness *is* coming from the pool after all! We've got to tell everyone, stop them from drinking the water!"

"I'll go and tell Runner!" Dasher turned and sprinted back up the slope, and Leaf followed, heading for the closest group of pandas, excitement pounding in her heart with every step. As she moved away from the pool, a soft breeze seemed to weave around her, bearing her forward. It was warm.

Despite the solemn news of the poisoned pool, she found herself smiling, then beaming.

The Great Dragon had heard her after all. It was all real. She was exactly where she was supposed to be.

CHAPTER ELEVEN

RAIN SAT ON THE edge of a high rock, holding a long bamboo cane in her paws, looking out over the sparse hills of the Northern Forest below her. The river sparkled in the distance between the hills, and the sun was warm on her fur. She finally felt as if the mountain chill had left her bones. She peeled the green outer bark from the bamboo and chewed on it, and it was refreshing and delicious. She was alone, responsible for nobody but herself, and well on her way back to the Prosperhill to expose Sunset for the fraud he was. Everything was just as it should be.

So why did she have the feeling something wasn't quite right?

It had been going on since Gray Light that morning—a sensation of being watched.

She chewed and chewed on the bamboo, her ears pricked,

the fur on the back of her neck standing on edge. There were sounds from the trees around her, but nothing she could definitively say was out of place—there were birds taking flight and landing, branches and leaves fluttering in the breeze.

She yawned and lay down on her back, still holding the bamboo over her chest, trying to give the impression that she was simply thinking about napping. In fact she scanned the undergrowth all around her, searching it from her upside-down vantage point, looking for any movement, for eyes watching from the shadows. But there was nothing there.

She sat back up with a humph.

Maybe she was imagining it.

After all, she was traveling alone through unfamiliar territory, with nobody to talk to since she'd given Plum the slip. It was natural to feel a little on edge. At one point she had even imagined it might be Plum catching up to her. Perhaps the only thing catching up to her was guilt. . . .

No, she told herself. *I've got nothing to feel guilty for.*

"She'll be fine alone, and so will I," she said aloud, getting to her paws.

Who would even be following her, anyway?

Answers to that question came much too easily. *Shadowhunter. Or the golden monkeys, somehow. Or another spy of Sunset's. Or some other predator I haven't even seen.*

Then she turned and tossed the last of her bamboo into the nearby bushes, in case there was anything there to scare off. But nothing moved.

"Fine," she said again, and set off to clamber down the steep slope, almost a cliff, between her and a gentler hillside below. Moss and vines hung from the edges of the rocks, and she dug her claws into patches of earth that shifted underneath her, but with a slightly clumsy sliding thump she made it down onto the softer ground. There was another advantage to taking the direct route down—if anything *were* following her, it'd either have to climb down too, in which case she'd see it, or it would be forced to go a long way around and possibly lose her trail. Satisfied with the cleverness of this thinking, she set off, casting looks back every so often just in case there was a shadowy creature climbing down the cliff. She didn't see anything.

She knew where she was heading now—she would go to the river, by the quickest and most direct route she could manage, and once she was there she would walk until she found some way of getting across. Even if it took her days, or longer. Even if she had to make a path herself. She'd had plenty of time to think about it on her journey: She would need to chew through the trunks of trees—small ones, but lots of them—and fetch the largest stones she could push, and slowly she would block up the river, at least enough to change the currents a little so she could swim across.

She knew it wasn't very likely this would work, but she also knew she was going to have to make a choice between that and swimming across. Would she be good enough to make it? Part of her said yes, obviously she'd make it. She'd done it once, hadn't she? But another part of her knew that she'd only survived because she'd gotten incredibly lucky—or because of the Dragon's help, as Leaf would've put it. Either way, she was on her own now, and in the face of the swollen river and its deadly currents, self-confidence could be a terrible mistake.

Something rustled in a tree above Rain's head, and she stumbled to a halt, looking up.

It was just a bird—it had to be. She couldn't see it, but she saw the branch moving where it must have flown away.

Her heart beating a little faster, she walked on. She would never get home if she stopped every time something moved in the forest. She was imagining it all. There was nothing watching her.

She focused on her goal. Get to the Prosperhill, and tell the pandas what Sunset had done. She rehearsed the words over and over in her mind:

Sunset Deepwood is a fraud and a traitor.

The Dragon Speaker tried to drown me.

No: *The Dragon Speaker tried to murder me.* That was better.

He's been working with the monkeys. . . . But she still didn't know why he wanted the striped bamboo, or what he had promised them in return, so that would only lead to questions she couldn't answer.

He made a deal with Brawnshanks to beat up Maple, just a tiny cub, and ask him all sorts of weird questions.

Maple could confirm that one—or at least he could say that the monkeys had bothered him in the night.

He's not the real Dragon Speaker! Again, she was certain of that, but how could she prove it? She picked up her pace a little. The longer she was away, the longer he would have spent working on the Prosperhill pandas, feeding them nonsense prophecies that were just vague enough to always come true.

Part of her—a small part, which she stamped down quickly—did wonder if she would have a better chance if she were able to say to them, *He's not the real Dragon Speaker; I am.*

But she wasn't going to lie about it. She'd fight him on her own terms, and she would win. Somehow . . .

Twigs snapped behind her, and she forced herself to ignore them, to keep her eyes focused forward and keep on walking. There was nothing there. She could easily imagine the pacing feet of a tiger, or the scampering of monkeys in the branches over her head, but that was all it was: imagination.

Yet she felt her shoulders tense, her walk get stiffer. She was so jittery that when something flashed between the trees just to her left, she missed her footing and slid gracelessly several bear-lengths down the slope. She scrambled for a paw hold and then looked around.

She'd seen it. And yet she hadn't—just a movement, fast and unmistakable. Just a bird?

No . . . there was the rustling again.

This wasn't just the forest.

Something was here with her.

Anger filled her, and for a moment she thought about standing her ground and facing her pursuer. But the ground she was on sloped sharply, punctuated by rocks and trees but mostly just soft moss and crunchy fallen leaves. She couldn't fight anything if she couldn't get a grip on the ground.

She had to run. Maybe she could lose it. Taking a deep breath, she launched herself into a slipping, sliding descent, using the tree trunks to slow herself down or bounce off. She reached the bottom of the slope, tripped over a rock, and went sprawling in a rolling heap, but she couldn't stop. She got up, shook herself, and ran along the bottom of what turned out to be a thin valley floor, only a few bear-lengths across, winding between more steep slopes or sharp rock cliffs that towered over her. Her heart started to pound in her throat as she realized that the valley might come to a sudden end at a cliff and she would have to climb. . . .

But she got lucky. The valley ended in a small, rocky upward slope that provided plenty of paw holds. Rain paused at the top for a few deep breaths, then ran on, weaving between trees and pushing through bushes. She had no idea if the thing was still following her. She refused to look back or slow her pace, until her breath was rasping painfully in her chest and her legs ached from keeping her balance on the rocky, meandering ground.

At the end of the next ridge she came to a soft shelf of grassy earth with a fallen tree on one side, and stumbled to a halt. She couldn't go any farther without a proper rest. She spun around, wondering if she ought to climb a tree to sleep, but she wasn't sure if even that would help if her pursuer caught up with her.

As she looked around for somewhere to hide, her gaze fell

on the fallen tree. It had a peculiar shape, darker at the broken end than she would have expected.

It's hollow! she thought, trotting over and sniffing at the inside of the log. It was just big enough that a young panda could crawl inside and turn around, and it would make a great hiding place.

Her aching muscles complained at her as she wriggled inside, but once she was in, the confined space reminded her of lying under Peony's fur as a cub. She rested her muzzle on her front paws and let out a long, tired sigh.

There was probably nobody after her. Even if there were, she'd probably lost them.

She still lay awake in the hollow tree for some time, her ears picking up every small noise that passed by, but finally she realized her eyes had drifted closed, and a moment later she was fast asleep.

Tap. Tap-tap.

Rain's eyes burst open, her heart hammering in her throat. What was that sound?

Tap-tap.

She could see out through the end of the log. It was still daytime, the green ferns bright and wavering in a soft breeze. But something was wrong.

Tap-tap. Tap-tap-tap.

Had the hollow log shifted then, just a little? The tapping sound was irregular, and coming closer, as if . . .

Rain tried to stay perfectly still, but she couldn't help cringing a little as she realized that the tapping was the sound of something on top of the log, moving slowly up it. The taps came closer and closer to her head, and now she could hear a slight scrape as the thing moved. The sound of paws on old bark . . .

Was it the thing that had been following her? Did it *know* it was standing right on top of her?

She held completely still for what felt like a very long time, breathing as softly as she could.

Just go away, she thought. *Whatever you are, just leave. . . .*

But the thing showed no sign of leaving. Whenever she thought it might have left, she would hear more tapping and shuffling up and down the log.

Her heart beat faster and faster, until her fear was so strong it started to turn into anger.

She wasn't going to lie here and hide anymore. She'd had enough of this!

She bunched her muscles and, with a burst of nervous energy, pushed her way out of the log and wheeled around, growling, to face whatever creature had been tapping up and down it.

She'd expected a monkey, or at least a red panda or a big bird of prey. But she found herself looking into the long red-and-black face and beady eyes of a crane. The bird turned its head to look at her and ruffled its feathers with a humph of displeasure.

Rain stared at it, and then looked around, wondering if the real threat might be lurking somewhere nearby. But there was no sign of any other creature on the ridge.

It was just a bird! Surely this wasn't the shadowy presence that had been following her all day. Her temper flared and she snapped at it, annoyed at herself as much as the crane. But the bird didn't move. It stared right at her.

"Get out of here!" she barked, but the crane still didn't move. "I don't believe—have you been following me?" she demanded. "What do you want?"

The crane took a few steps toward her and lowered its head in what was either a long, critical look or a kind of bow of greeting, Rain wasn't quite sure. The red markings on the top of its head looked just like a gingko leaf. Then it opened its beak and squawked something.

"Look, I don't know how to speak Bird," Rain said. "Sorry. But you've got to stop following me!"

The bird squawked again and hopped down from the log. It took a few steps across the grass toward Rain, and Rain backed away.

"Do you not understand Panda?" Rain muttered. "I suppose there's no reason you would. *Go. Away.*" She raised a paw and, quite slowly, not actually wanting to hurt the stupid crane, swiped her claws through the air. She'd given the bird plenty of time to get out of the way, and sure enough it took to the sky in a flutter of large white-and-black feathers. But instead of wheeling away, it landed in the nearest tree and went on watching Rain.

Rain sniffed. This was ridiculous. She wasn't going to be afraid of a spindle-legged bird. "Well, you can keep staring if you like. *I'm* going to get some more sleep. And if you or anyone else disturbs me . . ." She remembered it couldn't understand her, bared her teeth, and growled.

The crane just watched her impassively.

"All right, then. I hope we understand one another," Rain said. She huffily wriggled back inside the hollow tree and curled up again, this time a bit closer to the opening. She couldn't see the crane from here. She shut her eyes and put her paws over her muzzle.

It took her even longer to get to sleep this time—she wasn't quite as exhausted, and she wasn't particularly relaxed, either, with her annoyance at the bird's weird behavior and how much it had frightened her running around her mind. But eventually she managed to nap, drifting in and out of wakefulness.

She finally opened her eyes and felt refreshed. The crane must have left by now. It wouldn't have stayed put just to watch a log with a sleeping panda in it. She crawled out of the tree and stretched.

She turned and yelped as she saw the crane. It was sitting on the ground right beside the log, preening its feathers.

"You're still here?" she snarled. The crane chirped a reply. "All right. I'm leaving. Don't follow me."

She turned and stomped away, sniffing the ground to see if she could find any bamboo to eat. It must be nearly Long

Light now, and she hadn't feasted properly since Golden Light. She peered out and spotted some growing on the next hill over, and headed for it, clambering down the hill she stood on without looking back at the crane. Maybe if she didn't look or say anything, it would finally get bored and leave.

A moment later there was the sound of large wings beating the air. Rain growled to herself but forced herself not to look. She refused to pay the stupid bird any attention. She climbed down and across another fallen tree and then up the next hill, until she reached a perch where bamboo grew up around the base of a small rock. She still didn't look. She climbed up onto the rock and sat down to break off one of the bamboo canes.

The crane landed beside the rock. It sat looking away from Rain this time, almost as if it was standing guard, though there was nothing of any interest in the direction it was pointing.

Rain sighed, and picked the leaves off the bamboo cane as quickly as she could.

"Great Dragon, at the Feast of Long Light your humble pandas bow before you; thank you for the gift of the bamboo and the endurance you bestow upon us," she said, all in one breath, before biting the ends off the leaves. The crane bowed its head again and started scratching at the ground. A moment later it had come up with a worm grasped in its beak, and it swallowed it down in one gulp.

Is it . . . feasting with me? Rain thought. *No. Cranes need to eat too. Must be a coincidence,* she supposed, as she hurried to finish her feast.

She wasn't at all surprised when the crane leaped into the sky once more as she climbed down from the rock and continued on her way. It annoyed her as she walked, trying to keep her nose pointed toward the distant river, to know that the crane was always nearby, even when she couldn't see it. But she was already starting to think there was nothing she could do to make it stop.

When she paused to drink from a brook running down the side of a hill, the bird was soon standing in the water downstream, splashing its feathers and looking pleased with itself. When she stopped for the Feast of Dying Light and then lay down for another nap, she saw it take a perch in the branches of a tree, and when she woke up she wasn't at all surprised to see it still sitting there.

"I wish I did speak Bird," she told it, "so you could tell me what you want, and I could tell you to buzz off."

She tried to sneak away and continue her journey while it was still dark, but even then, she looked up to see the full moon flicker as the shadow of a long-necked bird soared over it.

"Maybe you're just lonely?" she asked the crane later, as she sat in the shade of a gingko tree to eat her Feast of Gray Light. "But there must be cranes near the river. We're nearly there now. You'll see. You won't want to follow me where I'm going after that."

The crane chirped in answer, and Rain sighed. Why did she bother?

She'd been right about the river. It was close now, and

before Sun Climb she could hear the sound of it rushing along somewhere below her. She was just starting to think that it seemed a long way below her, farther than she'd expected, when she reached the edge of a tree line and found herself on a kind of headland, looking down at a long drop to the glittering water. The river bent around the hill she was standing on, meaning it was a steep clamber down twenty or maybe thirty bear-lengths to the riverbank on all three sides.

The crane circled overhead and then landed on the edge, looking down at the difficult climb. It looked at Rain, looked back at the side of the hill, and then made a sound that Rain thought sounded dubious. She scowled at the bird.

"Well, we can't all fly, can we? Go on, buzz off, Stick Legs." She head-butted the crane's perch, making it shift over with a startled flap of its wings. Then she looked down at the descent.

It was less steep than a cliff, but steeper than a slope. She'd be able to walk parts of it on her four paws, following a path that clung to the edge. Other places she'd have to let herself down by her claws.

If she chose not to take this path, though, she'd have to walk back into the woods and find another way around, and she was sick and tired of walking and of thinking she was finally close to the river and then discovering it was still beyond the next hill. If she did this right, she would land with her paws on the bank. It was worth it.

I wish I had Leaf's climbing skills right now, she thought, turning to let herself down onto the path, back paws first. She'd never gone much higher than the first comfortable branch of any tree. Except, of course, the column of rock where she'd found the monkeys' striped bamboo.

Thinking about that bamboo gave her a burst of determination. She'd made it to the top of the column and back down, hadn't she? Plus, if she didn't get back across the river, she would never find out what kind of deal Sunset and Brawnshanks had made.

She lowered herself onto the ledge and then carefully brought her front paws down onto it. It was steep and slippery, but she managed to walk along it, pressing her side against the rock, until she couldn't go any farther and had to turn and let herself slide down, past a curtain of vines that tickled her nose, to another rock ledge. The system worked, though by the third time she'd had to lower herself down, her front legs were starting to ache and her chest fur was matted with mud and bits of twig and vine.

She stepped down onto another ledge and crept her way along it, almost losing her balance as she ducked her head aside to make room for a tree root that jutted out of the wall in front of her. There was a wide, flat rock just ahead, and she made for it, grateful that she'd be able to sit and catch her breath a little. But before she could get there, something white and black swept in front of her. She yelped, and had to crouch down low to the path and dig her claws into the earth to stop herself toppling over as the crane flapped at her, squawking and beating its wings in her face.

"What are you doing?" Rain yelled. "Get out of the way, you stupid creature! Are you trying to kill me?"

The crane went on squawking frantically, landing on the path in front of her and putting its wings out, blocking her way.

"What did I ever do to you, Stick Legs?" Rain snarled, backing up and hitting her head on the tree root. "Are you working for Sunset? Do you want to stop me getting back there? Well, tough!" She looked over the side. It would be a long slide down, but she could let herself over the edge of this rock, and if she sank her claws into the ground, she could slow her drop.

Sticking her tongue out at the flapping crane, she lowered her back paws over the edge, took a deep breath, and let go.

The slide was steeper and faster than she'd hoped, but when her back legs and then her bottom struck stone, she managed to hold on to her balance and not topple over and roll off the edge. She looked up at the crane.

It had moved along the path where she'd been planning to walk. As she was looking, it stuck one spindly leg out and, very deliberately, stepped onto the flat rock where Rain had thought she would take a nice rest.

The rock wobbled. Then it tipped over and fell. The crane leaped into the air and Rain watched, her jaws falling open, as the rock crashed and rolled down the hillside, kicking up showers of mud and taking other rocks and vines with it, until it dropped over an edge and plunged down a long drop to land in the mud below with a thud.

Slowly, Rain looked up into the sky. The crane was circling above her. It landed on a tree branch nearby, tilted its head, and let out a long "A-kaaaaa!"

Rain sagged into a sitting position on her small ledge, staring at the bird.

"What in the name of the Dragon just happened?" she whispered. "Did you know that rock was going to fall? Did you just . . . save my life?"

The bird said nothing in reply, but preened under its wing.

It *couldn't* be. Why would it do this? It had been following her for a whole day now—could it have known she would come here? How did it even know the rock wasn't safe?

The rest of the journey down the slope passed in a kind of blur. The crane stayed close but didn't interfere anymore. Rain finally landed, fur ruffled and muscles aching, in a patch of silty mud. She didn't even try to get up for several breaths, but just lay there and watched the crane hop from perch to perch and finally land in the mud beside her.

"You going to help me get across the river, too?" she asked it.

It let out a soft "A-kaa" in reply.

"Great," said Rain, and sat up, shaking off the worst of the mud and looking around for the edge of the water. But although she could hear the rushing of the river, she didn't immediately see it. Instead of the kind of riverbank she was used to, where the trees and bushes and rocks went right up into the edge of the water, she was standing on a long silt bank with a few weeds and rocks poking up out of it.

She followed the sound of the river, slipping and sliding as the bank sloped down sharply, until she found herself standing at the edge of the water, among dead reeds and white rocks, looking across at the other side.

It was closer than it had been. Much closer.

Rain's eyes widened and her heart started to pound as she looked across and saw that for a few bear-lengths the opposite bank seemed wet and muddy too, and then the familiar deep green of thick bushes and mossy rocks started again.

"The flood," she gasped to the crane, which had flown forward to stand with its sticklike legs in the gently flowing river. "It's finally over! The water level's gone down. The currents will be different. I can swim across!" She splashed into the water a few paces and rolled over, washing the mud from her fur and coming up near the crane in a shower of droplets. "You see, Stick Legs? I'm going home!"

CHAPTER TWELVE

"APPROACH, FRIENDS," SAID SUNSET. He was sitting on a rock at the edge of the feast clearing, and Ghost was sitting on the ground right beside him, feeling prouder and more at home than he had since the night that the Snow Cat had shown him its footprints and led the leopards to catch that deer. Sunset himself had asked if Ghost would sit at his left paw, while Blossom and Ginseng sat on his right. This was how he'd chosen to receive the questions of the creatures of the Bamboo Kingdom.

They'd been sending out word for a couple of days. Every time they met a squirrel or a monkey or a takin, the pandas told them to tell their friends that the Dragon Speaker would meet them and hear them on this day, at High Sun. Now there were a number of animals climbing the hill to the feast clearing. Three golden takins lumbered up the path, their long fur gleaming in the bright sunshine. A solitary manul cat about half the size of Shiver sat at the edge of the clearing, grooming its fluffy gray-and-brown fur and casting suspicious glances at the assembled pandas.

Sunset held the blue Dragon Speaker stone in his paw as one by one they approached him. Some of them bowed before they spoke, like the small family of pikas—mouse-like creatures with fluffy round bodies—that scurried right up to the rock where he sat. The pikas pressed their noses to the ground, and two of them left them there even when the third began to speak.

"Oh, great Dragon Speaker!" she squeaked. "It is an honor and a privilege to be able to speak with you! Please ask the Dragon to bless our humble family!"

The others trembled as if in agreement.

"Bless you all," Sunset said. "The Dragon itself is blessed to have such followers as you. Do you have a question for your Dragon Speaker?"

The pika who had spoken nudged her companion, who lifted his head nervously.

"We lost our burrow in the flood," he said. "Now the waters have gone down, but the burrow was washed away. Should we return to the bank? Or should we stay up on higher ground?"

Sunset nodded, and held out his blue stone for all to see. He closed his eyes, and his head fell back. For a moment there was perfect silence in the crowded clearing. All eyes were on him, including Ghost's.

Then he opened his eyes with a small gasp. He looked down at the pikas and smiled.

"The Dragon wants you to know that your choices are your own," he said. "But if you return to the riverbank, you will be safe there. The flood is over. The water will not rise again."

A chittering and sighing of relief ran around the feast clearing, pandas nodding solemnly as monkeys whooped and takins turned and lowed to each other in soft, happy voices. The pikas backed away, still bowing, their small noses practically dragging on the floor.

The next to approach was the group of takins, and they had a similar set of questions. Was it safe to graze near the water? Sunset repeated that yes, it was safe. The oldest of the takins raised her drooping head and asked, in a quavering voice, if the Dragon knew whether her mate was safe, as he too had been lost in the flood. Ghost realized that most, if not all, of these creatures probably had the same story—something had been lost; someone had died.

Sunset looked at the takin for a few long moments before holding the stone out once more.

"I'm sorry," he said with a heavy sigh as his eyes opened. "I believe your mate is lost for good. The Dragon tells us that when there is no hope for one, we must cling all the more to another—these, your calves, will take care of you."

The two younger takins nodded in their slow way, and nuzzled their mother's golden fur comfortingly.

The next creature that came to Sunset's rock was the manul cat. Ghost noticed several of the pandas around the clearing frowning. Pebble was sitting closest to Ghost, and Ghost whispered to him, "What's everyone worried about?"

"The Dragon Speaker was attacked by a manul clan while he was lost after the flood," Pebble whispered back.

But when Ghost looked back up at Sunset, the Dragon Speaker showed no fear or anger. Ghost felt a new rush of respect for him—he wasn't sure that if he'd been attacked by a gang of these angry-faced fur balls he would have been able to sit there quite so calmly, even if this particular cat had had nothing to do with it.

"Dragon Speaker," meowed the manul, sitting up straight with her tail tucked neatly across her paws. "I too come to you for answers. Not from the Dragon, but from you."

"Ask me your questions, my friend," Sunset said mildly.

"Why did the flood happen? And why didn't the pandas warn us about it in time? Where were you, when we lost homes and loved ones?"

A scandalized chatter ran around the clearing. It seemed that the cat had hit a nerve.

"Didn't take long," muttered one voice that Ghost couldn't pinpoint in the crowd.

"Rude," said the elderly takin, shaking her golden head.

". . . didn't think she'd just come out and *say* it," Ghost heard one of the pikas chitter.

"Shh!" replied one of the others, its ears pressing back against its head. "I want to hear the answer."

The manul cat didn't seem bothered by the commotion she'd provoked. She sat completely still, her powerful gaze never leaving Sunset's face.

Sunset held up his paw for quiet, and a hush came over the assembled animals.

"My friends. My lady manul," he said, nodding to the cat but addressing the whole clearing. "I know these are questions that many of you have harbored for a long time, that have weighed on you. I know that you may have felt betrayed by us—by me in particular. The Dragon Speaker is supposed to keep the whole kingdom safe, and in this way, I failed you."

There was another soft murmuring that quickly died away as Sunset got to his paws.

"The facts are these: the pandas did not warn you of the flood, because they were not warned either. I was not warned."

More shocked noises from the animals in the crowd. Ghost frowned as he watched Sunset hang his head sadly. Why would the Dragon do this?

"I do not know exactly what happened," Sunset went on. "The Dragon hides this knowledge from me, even now—but I think that something disturbed the balance of this world. Perhaps it was a single unthinkable deed, or perhaps we all contributed to it in our own ways, and we must be extra careful to follow the Dragon's instructions from now on. But whatever terrible thing was done, it caused that break with the Dragon's sight, as surely as it caused the flood to come down upon us."

He paused, allowing this news to sink in. Ghost's mind was racing. Something had caused the flood, something some creature had done that was so against the balance of the world . . . but what could it have been? Could any one creature have that much power? And if so, how could they stop such a thing from happening again?

"I thank you from the bottom of my heart, my lady manul, for your forthrightness and for bringing these questions out into the open," Sunset went on, with a small bow to the cat in front of him. "I have dedicated the last year of my wanderings to searching for the answers to them, yet the mystery remains. But I can promise you this: if I find that there are creatures whose presence is responsible for this terrible event, they will answer for what they have done."

The clearing was silent for a moment; then several of the pandas roared out a cheer. "Thank you, Dragon Speaker! Thank you, Sunset!"

Other animals took up the call, and all of a sudden the air was filled with hooting and chittering. Ghost roared his approval along with them. It felt wonderful to be sitting by Sunset's side as the creatures of the Bamboo Kingdom came together to lend him their support.

The manul cat didn't cheer. Ghost saw her eyes narrow a

little before she dipped a graceful bow and turned, tail swishing behind her, to walk away. Ghost sighed. The *whole* Bamboo Kingdom clearly wasn't quite convinced. He didn't know what more the cat wanted. Sunset had explained it all, answered all her questions. Some creatures were just ungrateful.

As the noise calmed down, Ghost spotted another furry shape at the edge of the clearing, up in a tree. It was Shiver. Her long white tail hung down from the branch where she lay, watching the proceedings with a look on her face that Ghost recognized from their long hunting trips through the mountains. It was the face she made when she'd spotted prey but wasn't sure she'd be able to catch it.

"Thank you all so much," Sunset declared, holding up his paws. "Thank you for bringing me your concerns and your questions. I am tired now, and this session is over, but please spread the word far and wide—I will speak to you all again soon."

There was another ragged cheer, and then the animals began to disperse, and Sunset climbed down from the rock and retreated from the group. Blossom and Ginseng moved to stand between him and the others, to make sure they gave him space to rest.

Ghost hurried over to Shiver's tree and climbed up to sit on the branch beside hers.

"I'm glad you came!" he said. He couldn't reach her to lick her face, but he blinked happily at her.

"Me too," said Shiver, but she wasn't smiling. A chill crept over the back of Ghost's neck. "He didn't really explain much, did he?"

Ghost stared at her. Hadn't she been listening? "What do you mean? He told us everything!"

Shiver's tail twitched in agitation. "Well, he used a lot of words. But he mostly just said that he didn't know."

"It's not his fault that he doesn't know *all* the answers," Ghost muttered. He felt himself sagging as he spoke to Shiver, resentment burning in his throat. She ought to have more faith in Sunset, but he knew deep down that that wasn't what hurt most about her attitude.

Hadn't she thought it was good that he was sitting by Sunset's left paw, that he'd found his place in this world at last? Hadn't she been even a little bit impressed?

"I think he knows more than he's letting on," he said, thinking of the mission that had been interrupted by the tiger. Sunset had said something about triplets. Could they be the ones responsible for the flood, after all? He wanted to explain this to Shiver—maybe then she'd understand that he had a role here now, that Sunset trusted him, and how much that meant to him. But instead he just said, "The Great Dragon will reveal more to him when it's ready. We just need to have faith."

"Faith? The Great Dragon?" Shiver said, looking at him sharply. "What about the Snow Cat? Where are its paws in all of this? Are you forgetting about *our* faith already?"

"No, of course not," Ghost said, but guilt pricked at his

paws. Perhaps he had forgotten, a tiny bit, in all of his eagerness to find a place for himself in the world of the Great Dragon.

"I just think Mother would be sad you don't thank the Snow Cat anymore," Shiver sniffed.

That's not fair, Ghost thought. But perhaps it was. The mention of Winter made his heart hurt, but he liked it here, where it was warm, and there was plenty of bamboo, and Sunset, at least, seemed to value his company. Why didn't Shiver like Sunset as much as he did?

Before he could figure out what to say to Shiver, he realized that something was going on below them in the clearing. A group of pandas had approached Sunset's napping spot and said something to Ginseng, who said something to Blossom.

Then Ghost's eyes landed on what the pandas had brought with them, and without another word to Shiver he started to climb down from the tree.

It was a panda—another new one he'd never seen before. This one was a young male, about the same age as Ghost, or maybe a little younger, but noticeably smaller. He seemed to be alone, with no parents or siblings, but he walked with a curious confidence, very unlike Goby's and Vine's nervous excitement when they had first arrived.

Ghost hurried over just as Ginseng roused Sunset from his nap. Sunset's ears pricked up as he listened to Ginseng, and then he stepped forward.

"How wonderful," Sunset said. "Another addition to our

family! Hello, young cub. My name is Sunset Deepwood. I am the Dragon Speaker. What's your name?"

"Pepper," said the new panda. "I used to be Pepper Tallcrag, but I guess now I'm Pepper Prosperhill."

"And very welcome you are," chuckled Sunset.

"We found him alone, near the river," said Cypress, who had entered the clearing with Pepper at his heels.

"You have no family?" Sunset asked.

"We got separated," said Pepper. "But you might have found my siblings? There were three of us. I'm a triplet."

Ghost froze where he stood, then sat down with a thump next to Pebble, who'd also come close to hear the new panda's story.

Several of the pandas made astonished, impressed noises. Pebble looked at Ghost.

"That's amazing!" he said. "Panda triplets are so rare! I've never heard of all three surviving before."

"Wow," said Ghost softly. He couldn't tell Pebble that he already knew this. He'd have to explain how he knew, and he'd promised Sunset. . . .

Sunset only stared at Pepper for a moment, then bowed to him smoothly. "How amazing," he said. "I'm afraid we haven't met any other triplets yet, but I promise you we will do our best to make sure you're reunited." Then he raised his head and called out to all the pandas, "My friends, please welcome Pepper Prosperhill, and make sure he is comfortable and wants for nothing."

"Welcome, Pepper!" chorused the pandas.

"Ghost, Pebble, why don't you take Pepper and show him around the Prosperhill a little?" Sunset said. Ghost's heart leaped at the responsibility, and he saw Pebble's eyes brighten, too. They hurried over to Pepper and introduced themselves.

"You'll soon fit in," said Pebble. "We'll show you where the best bamboo grows, and where we all sleep."

"I can't wait," said Pepper. He dipped his head, a little sadly. "It'll be nice to be with pandas my age again. I've been wandering for so long. I miss my two siblings."

"Yeah," said Pebble kindly. "I know the feeling."

Ghost bowed his head, thinking about the brother Pebble had said he'd lost in the flood. "Me too," he said. Pebble looked curiously at him, and Ghost realized he hadn't really talked to Pebble about Snowstorm and Frost. He'd been focused on fitting in here, and on trying to make sure Shiver did too. As they turned to walk from the clearing, he started to talk. "I left two siblings behind—they're alive, but I don't know if I'll ever see them again. They're still in our old territory, in the White Spine—"

"Ghost," Sunset's voice cut in. Ghost looked around and saw the Dragon Speaker calling him back.

"Hang on," he told the others, and trotted over to where Sunset stood, once more a little way apart from the rest of the pandas. He passed by Blossom and Ginseng, and they both gave him slightly suspicious looks, but they didn't stop him.

"Ghost, you must be careful," Sunset said under his breath,

when Ghost was close enough to hear. "Don't tell that cub too much about yourself."

"Oh—but why?" Ghost asked.

"Because you must get *him* talking. Make him tell you everything he knows. You remember I mentioned triplets to you?"

"Of course," Ghost murmured.

"The truth is, the Dragon *warned* me about the triplets," Sunset whispered. "It told me, long ago, that one day panda triplets would try to take over the Bamboo Kingdom! They are destined to overthrow the Dragon Speakers, to murder me, and rule over all with an evil paw. I know it's hard to believe of a cub," he added. "But this cub is going to grow up to be very, very dangerous. Already I suspect he is not telling the whole truth. Either way, his presence poses a great danger, not just to me personally, but to the whole kingdom, even to the Dragon itself."

Ghost didn't know what to say. Sunset was right: it *was* hard to believe that the pleasant, confident young panda he'd just met could be secretly plotting to kill his friend. But the Great Dragon knew everything, didn't it?

Maybe it warned us so early because there's still hope, Ghost thought. *Maybe Pepper can be turned back to the side of the Dragon Speakers!*

"Look after him, just as I've told you," Sunset went on. "Become his friend, if you can. But you *must* find out what his reasons are for coming here, and where the other two triplets are now. Understand?"

"Yes! I will!" Ghost gasped.

"Thank you, Ghost. I knew as soon as I met you that you would have a role to play in all of this. You've already proven yourself to be loyal. Now I trust you with the most important task of your life, and if you do it well . . . then, just perhaps, you and I may save the whole Bamboo Kingdom."

CHAPTER THIRTEEN

"THIS TIGER HAS THE worst timing," Rain growled. She peered through the ferns where she'd scrambled to try to avoid Shadowhunter as soon as she'd smelled him coming. She wasn't sure it would be much use—he'd probably scent her, too, any minute now.

She had walked a little way along the riverbank, searching for something familiar on the opposite side, so that she wouldn't be too lost after she crossed the river. It had been a mistake—if she'd swum across immediately, she'd be heading back to the Prosperhill right now, instead of trying to avoid a tiger who could probably see, smell, and hear better than she could.

She could see his stripy tail lashing in a patch of sunlight a little way away. If he kept on walking, there was a good chance she could slip into the river and swim across before he turned back. But she didn't want to make a noise until she was absolutely sure he was gone.

She didn't exactly think that he would eat her, no matter what she'd told Leaf. But she wasn't sure he was a friend, either. He was definitely a complication that she didn't want in her life right now. She was certain he would not be happy that she'd given Leaf and Plum the slip. He might try to force her to go and find them, and she might have to explain about what had happened on the mountain, and either way it would bring the entire Dragon Speaker thing back up and she just didn't want to. She had her own mission, and she was going to get it done, no matter what.

What was he doing down here anyway?

She told herself she didn't care. He was wrong about her, so whatever it was, it didn't concern her.

But actually, she was a little concerned. So far she had only seen him pacing back and forth, watching the southern bank.

The black-necked crane was standing peacefully in the water a few bear-lengths away, looking like any old bird minding its own business.

The tiger turned, its tail lashing behind it, and Rain cringed back. It had smelled her. It was coming—

But then she heard the breaking of twigs and creaking of branches, and a screeching sound drawing closer and closer. She looked up to see a small troop of golden monkeys fly through the trees overhead. When she glanced over at the tiger again, it had vanished into the undergrowth.

The monkeys didn't seem to spot Rain, but came to a bouncing, chattering halt in a tree not far from her hiding spot.

"Patience!" one of them snapped to the others. "I told you, we're waiting!"

"I hate waiting," another one spat. She dropped off the branch, and Rain thought she might plummet into the bushes, but she caught herself with her back paws at the last minute and swung there, upside down.

"Why did you volunteer to come here, then?" chuckled another.

Some of the monkeys were familiar, Rain realized. They were definitely Brawnshanks's troop. Two of them had been there when she'd followed them to the column of rock where the striped bamboo grew. One of them was the small one who'd climbed right to the top of the bouncing canes. What had she been called? Nimbletail?

"Brawnshanks said to go across and wait," Nimbletail said. "You thought it wouldn't involve waiting?"

"Not *all day*," said the upside-down monkey, scratching her chin.

Brawnshanks sent them across the river, Rain thought. *But what are they waiting for?*

Whatever it was, they were much too close, and if the tiger was watching them, there was an even greater chance it'd spot her too. Moving was risky, but she couldn't just stay here and wait for them to notice her.

Slowly, carefully, she tried to back out of her ferns.

But she timed it badly. The impatient monkey hanging from the tree branch turned slightly, and then let out a shriek of surprise.

"What's that?"

"It was nothing," yawned one of the others.

"Shut up! I mean it—I saw something move!"

Rain didn't waste any more time. She was off and running while the monkeys were still talking, and she was only just quick enough—after a few paces she heard the sound of hooting monkeys leaping onto tree branches just behind her.

She couldn't outrun them. She had to find a better place to hide, and *quick*. She skidded around a large rock and spotted a thick bush on the other side. She crawled underneath, as deep as she could, and then pressed her belly to the ground and tried not to breathe.

"Where is it?" screeched the impatient monkey, from the branches up above her.

"What was it? Panda? That big white cat?" said another. Rain cringed as she realized he had stopped right on the rock beside her hiding place.

White cat? she thought. *That's not Shadowhunter. . . .*

"Not sure," said the monkey.

"We can't go back to Brawnshanks and tell him we think we saw something but we're not sure!" snapped the male on the rock. "Can't have gone far—fan out and find it!"

Rain heard the sound of four or five monkeys leaping down onto the ground, and held herself as still as she could. If she was lucky . . .

She wasn't lucky. Before she could even finish the thought, the young female Nimbletail passed by her bush, her long tail curled behind her, and immediately peered under the leaves.

Her eyes met Rain's. Rain tensed, ready to spring. But the monkey didn't call out to the others. She just stared. Her eyes narrowed in confusion. Had she recognized Rain? Why wasn't she saying anything?

"Nimbletail!" yelled the impatient female, making both of them jump. "What've you found?"

"I . . . can't see. Too dark," said Nimbletail.

Wait, what?

"Let me have a look," said the other female. Nimbletail winced, and then another monkey face appeared at the edge of the bush. This one frowned too, but then crowed, "Aha! There you are, little panda! Are you blind? She's right there!" she added, turning to shove Nimbletail.

Rain didn't wait any longer. She burst from the bush, swiping the female aside with a heavy paw.

"Get lost!" she roared, rearing back and turning to swat at the monkey on the rock too. He leaped out of the way, up into the tree with a high laugh.

"Brawnshanks'll enjoy this," he yelled. "Come on, let's tell him!"

Rain kept her teeth bared and her paw raised as the monkeys hopped and swung past her and into the branches. For a moment, she thought she saw Nimbletail pause and look back at her, an apologetic frown on her face. But then she was gone.

Rain stood by the side of the river, breathing hard, as the monkeys swung away downriver. They must be heading to a place where they could cross, now that the water level was lower—and the Prosperhill was probably near there.

She half expected to see Shadowhunter stalking out of the undergrowth to confront her—she had certainly made enough noise. But she stood there for another few long breaths, and there was no sign of the tiger. He must have run off in the opposite direction.

Hanging around was pointless. She had to get across the river. There wasn't exactly a shallow path right where she was standing, but she was sure she could swim across now that the currents weren't as swift and deadly. She waded out a few paw-lengths, feeling the lovely, familiar sensation of the water on her fur.

But suddenly, instead of the soft silty ground and thick reeds, she felt something jab into one of her paw pads. She yelped and pulled her paw back. *Must have been a rock.* She tried to go around it, but there was something long and smooth here, too. Carefully, she pushed the reeds aside and peered through the water.

They weren't rocks. They were bones.

She reeled back, her heart pounding, onto the safe, soft mud.

There were so many of them, and they were so . . . familiar. *I saw this,* she thought. *When I was in the river. When I was drowning. But I thought I was just dreaming; I never imagined that they were really there....*

The bones of the animals who'd drowned during the flood. She'd known it before, and she knew it now.

There were *so many*. She stared downriver, feeling strangely dizzy.

Her father's bones were here somewhere. She had no memory of him, but she knew he had fallen into the river and drowned. Pebble's brother, Stone, was probably here. Cypress's sister, Citrus. So many others.

Leaf would say this is a bad omen, she thought. *A warning from the Great Dragon.*

But to Rain, the water lapping around the bones seemed gentle, as if the river was taking care of them. Somehow, the sight wasn't gloomy. And she was sure her father wouldn't want her to stand here thinking about his death, not when she still had a job to do on the far shore.

She waded forward, stepping around the bones. Then she stopped in her tracks once again, as the black-necked crane swooped down and landed right in front of her.

"Oh, *now* you're here again?" she said. "Where were you when I needed a distraction a minute ago?" The crane croaked a quiet reply. It stood perfectly still in the water, staring at her. Rain sighed. "Well, I'm going over there. I imagine I'll see you on the far bank," she said, and sidestepped to go around the crane.

With deliberate slowness, the crane stepped in front of her

again and raised its wings, holding them out, blocking her path.

Rain looked at the crane, then at the opposite shore.

"Oh, come on!" she growled. "Not now!"

The crane gave one powerful flap of its wings, and Rain felt the pulse of air against her face. She stared the bird right in its beady eye.

"I *know*. It's dangerous," she said. "And I appreciate you helping me out earlier, even though I have no idea why you did it—and you were kind of creepy about it. But you're not going to stop me. I'm going *because* it's dangerous! I've got to save my mother and Pebble!"

She took a deep breath and barreled forward, right at the bird's chest. She thought it would get out of the way. Instead it reared back and pecked at her, hard, right behind the ear. She yelped and ducked aside, shocked despite herself, and as she did, the bird slammed its wing into her face with such force that she lost her footing and splashed full-length into the water.

She came back up, roaring and dripping water. No stick-legged bird was going to stop her getting back to her mother!

"Get off!" she roared, and swiped at the bird with one paw. This time the crane was forced to dodge, and it did, flapping up into the air with a squawk. Rain saw the opportunity and took it, gulping a big breath of air and diving forward and into the water. She swam as hard and as fast as she could, following the riverbed down, through clouds of algae and tangled reeds, scattering a shoal of glittering golden fish. She swam and swam until her lungs burned, feeling the tug of the current on her, letting it pull her downriver at the same time as she made for the opposite shore.

Just as she knew she would have to come up for air, she saw the riverbed beneath her start to slope up again. Her head burst through the surface and she gasped, and then laughed out loud, triumphant to find herself past the middle of the river. She let herself float to the surface for a moment, looking around for the crane. It was in the air now, a bright flash against the sky. Then it was gone. Rain fixed her eyes on the familiar bamboo-dotted slopes of the Southern Forest, and swam with all her might for the shore.

CHAPTER FOURTEEN

LEAF POUNDED ACROSS A rocky outcropping, her eyes fixed on the tall canes growing up between the cracks and wavering in the breeze. Was this red vein? Dasher had said it grew in places where other things wouldn't, and had gotten its name from the streaks running through its leaves. They had to find it. Runner Healing Heart had said it was the only bamboo that could help with the pain of a creature who'd drunk bad water. Every panda and red panda at the Clearpool was counting on them.

She seized the bamboo in her paw and pulled the cane down so she could inspect the leaves. They looked *kind of* red?

"Dash!" she yelled. "Is this it?"

Dasher's head popped up over the edge of the rock and he scampered to her side.

"No," he panted, shaking his head sadly. "Leaves are the wrong shape." He sank to his belly for a moment, and Leaf gave him an encouraging lick on the top of his head.

"You know so much about these things," she said. "We'll find some, I'm sure of it."

"It's not really that special," Dasher said, but she could tell he was pleased. "All red pandas know a bit about healing. We eat anything—we know not all of it's going to be good for us."

Still, it was Dasher who finally found the red-veined bamboo, a few lonely canes growing right out of the side of a cliff. Leaf climbed up and tore them out.

"This stuff will deal with the pain," Dasher said. "Now we just need to find some purple leaf. The two together should help. I hope."

"Maybe you should be a Healing Heart after all," Leaf said. Dasher chuckled tiredly and shook his head.

"Nah. I'm a Climbing Far for life."

Dasher could only carry one cane of the red bamboo in his jaws, so Leaf took the other three. They hurried on, awkwardly, the bamboo sometimes getting stuck in bushes or caught between the cracks of rocks.

"Purple leaf grows near water," Dasher reminded her. "And anything growing near that pool is probably bad news. So we need to find some other water."

As they walked, Leaf kept looking around, hoping for any sign that Aunt Plum and Rain might have found them. She longed for Plum's wisdom right now, not to mention her moral support. She still hadn't told the Clearpool pandas that she believed she was the new Dragon Speaker, and she wasn't sure how she was going to say it when she did. It would have helped to have Plum there to back her up.

She missed Rain, too, even though having her there probably wouldn't have helped in the slightest.

There was no sign of either of them, but as she was scanning the tree line, Leaf caught sight of something else. A bird taking flight, then another and another, rising from behind a clump of trees.

"Ducks!" she exclaimed. "And where there are ducks, there's water!"

"Let's go," Dasher said, and together they dragged their bamboo canes along the side of a hill, up and over another big rocky shelf, and finally through the trees. Sure enough, there it was—a little brook that burbled through the forest, just wide enough to sustain a small family of ducks and a couple of stands of purple bamboo.

They broke off as much as they could possibly carry. When their mouths were full and aching from keeping the canes held tight, Dasher plucked off pawfuls of the leaves and stuffed them in between his teeth.

By the time they made it back to the Clearpool pandas, Leaf thought her jaw might be about to fall off. She dropped the canes as soon as she could, sending a few of them scattering down the grassy hillside, and rubbed at her muzzle with her paws. But there wasn't any time to waste on her own aches and pains. She plucked leaves from the red-vein bamboo and the purple leaf, and ran to the tree where Hyacinth and Cane were still sprawled.

Hyacinth looked even weaker than she had before, and Cane's breathing had slowed almost to match hers.

"I'm back," she said. The cub stirred, but he didn't look up.

Trying to hold back her panic, Leaf tore the leaves into pieces as small as she could manage, and gently held them up to Hyacinth's nose.

"Please, try to eat," she said. "This will make you feel better, I promise it will. Please try. . . ."

Hyacinth's muzzle twitched, ever so slightly. Then it went still again. Leaf wanted to throw herself down in front of Hyacinth and beg her to eat, but she knew it wouldn't help. She had to stay calm, for Cane, for all the pandas she could feel watching. She swallowed hard and put her other front paw over Hyacinth's limp one.

"Great Dragon," she whispered. "At the Feast of Long Light your humble pandas bow before you. Thank you for the gift of this healing bamboo, and the endurance you bestow upon us."

Please, she thought. *Please endure, Hyacinth. . . .*

Hyacinth took a breath, stirring the leaves in front of her nose. Her tongue flicked out and licked them from Leaf's palm. Leaf held her breath. Hyacinth was barely able to chew, but eventually she swallowed.

Leaf let out a heavy sigh, and quickly tore more shreds and held them up to Hyacinth's mouth. This time the tongue came almost immediately. Leaf continued feeding the leaves to Hyacinth, pausing only to place a few in front of Cane. He sniffed at them and then, without opening his eyes, reached out his muzzle and swallowed them down. Leaf's heart was beating faster and faster, but with every mouthful, Hyacinth gained just a little energy, until finally her eyes peeled slowly open and she looked up.

"Leaf?" she croaked, her voice barely a whisper.

"It's me," Leaf beamed. "You're going to be all right."

"Let me take over," said a voice behind her. "You get some rest." It was Juniper. He didn't look well himself, but Leaf still let him take the bamboo canes from her and crack them open. She was suddenly exhausted, and flopped down in the soft grass.

The pandas and the red pandas gathered around, each of them eating a little of the two kinds of bamboo, the pandas crunching into the canes so that the red pandas could pull out the stringy green insides. Leaf felt Dasher sit down beside her and lean against her flank.

"Thank you both," said Runner Healing Heart, when all their friends had had at least a few mouthfuls of bamboo. "And thank the Great Dragon for sending you to us!"

Leaf and Dasher looked at each other.

"I think it's time," Dasher murmured.

Leaf nodded. Anxiety was twisting in her stomach, but she knew he was right.

Runner and a few of the pandas were staring at them now.

Leaf got stiffly to her paws, and cleared her throat.

"I have something to say," she said. All the pandas and red pandas who could turned to look at her. She took a few deep breaths. "I think that the Great Dragon did send us here," she said. "I had a vision, when I looked in the pool. That's how I knew it was poisoned. I saw it turn black. And it's not the first vision I've had. Because I . . . I am a Dragon Speaker."

Nobody said anything, for so long that Leaf almost wanted to take it back, just to break the silence. It sounded absurd, now that she heard herself say it out loud. Why would they believe her?

"Oh," said Crabapple. "Of *course*. Why didn't we see it before?"

Leaf blinked at him.

"That's right—you had the vision when we were lost on the mountain. You saw the Dragon!" said Hunter Leaping High. "And none of us realized what that meant!"

"Dragon Speaker!" Grass cried, and bowed her head. "We have a Dragon Speaker once more!"

Several of the other pandas bowed too. Leaf found herself struggling not to laugh out loud from sheer relief.

"There's nobody I'd rather have as my Dragon Speaker," said Seeker Climbing Far, hurrying forward and clasping Leaf's large paw between her tiny ones.

"You're good and honest. You'll be wonderful," croaked Hyacinth from her position still propped up against the tree.

"Hooray for Leaf!" squeaked Cane.

Leaf bowed her head. "It means so much that you all believe in me! I can't tell you how much. . . ." She had to stop and catch her breath, afraid she wouldn't be able to go on. "There's more, though. There's a change coming."

Where should she even start to explain about Shadowhunter, Aunt Plum, Rain, and the missing triplet?

She laid it out as simply as she could, and though the red pandas seemed a little upset when she described the days she had spent with the tiger—Shadowhunter had, after all, killed one of their own—they seemed to accept the rest of the story.

"I don't understand it all myself," she said at last. "But I know that I will always do my best for the Bamboo Kingdom, no matter what."

"Are you sure you're well enough for this?" Leaf asked, for the third time, as the little group of red pandas gathered around her. It had only been a day since she and Dasher had brought back the healing bamboo, and many of the pandas were still recovering. "Dasher and I can go by ourselves. . . ."

"Nonsense," said Wanderer. "We're well enough to walk in the woods and sniff for bats."

"You broke off your quest to help us," said Seeker. "We'll help you find the trail again. You must follow the Dragon's signs and find your sibling, for the sake of all the kingdom!"

Leaf flushed, pleased but actually a little bit intimidated by how seriously the red pandas were taking her story. What if it turned out the whole thing wasn't what she'd thought at all? The Dragon hadn't *told* her she'd find her triplet if she followed the bats; that was just a hunch she'd had.

But she was grateful, all the same. They headed off, fanning out in the direction of the gingko glade where she and Dasher had met Gale.

It had been a few days since they'd been there. Would there still be any trace of the trail? Leaf couldn't help hoping, as she sniffed around the tree where they'd slept and nosed through the undergrowth, searching for the smell of bats or their droppings. But perhaps it had rained, or the wind had dried any trace of them and blown it away, because there was nothing.

Sighing, she set off to find Dasher, who had gone farther afield. Then, as she was crossing an open space at the crest of a hill, she looked down and saw that the red pandas were all gathered together at the trunk of a tall tree.

Her heart began to race, and she hurried down the slope to the tree. She saw on the faces of the red pandas, before they even spoke, that they had found something.

"They roosted here!" Dasher exclaimed. "And recently. Their scent is all over this tree!"

"This way," said Wanderer, appearing around the tree, her stripy tail held high with excitement. The red pandas and Leaf scrambled to follow her, and she led them to the tree line and pointed out the scent, a few droppings on the trunks of trees. "They flew off in that direction. I'd bet my tail on it."

"What are you going to do now?" Seeker asked. Leaf and Dasher exchanged a look.

"I think I have to follow them," said Leaf.

"And I'm going with you," said Dasher. "Obviously."

Seeker nuzzled Dasher's chin. "Be safe, and come back soon."

"You won't stay at the Clearpool, will you?" said Leaf with concern.

"It is the Darkpool now," said Seeker. "No, Speaker Leaf. We will move on and find fresh water. Wherever we go, we know you'll find us."

"We will." Leaf stared into the forest. She had a direction again. The Dragon hadn't let her lose the trail. "I'll find the third triplet, and the three of us will fulfill our destiny. Wait and see."

CHAPTER FIFTEEN

"I'LL GET YOU!" GHOST put his head down and charged along the valley floor. He could see the black paws and stubby tail of his prey vanishing around a rock, and put on a burst of speed. But when he skidded around the corner, Pepper was gone.

"Boo!" cried a voice, and Ghost jumped, lost his balance, and fell down on his side as Pepper's head popped up behind the rock. Pepper let out a laugh so hard he fell back too, waving his legs in the air.

"All right, *you* got *me*," Ghost chuckled, getting to his paws. Pepper sat up and preened behind his ears.

Ghost smiled as he watched the young bear.

He *liked* Pepper. He was a little odd, but he was playful, and he had never questioned Ghost's white fur or his strange upbringing. Once again, a voice in the back of Ghost's mind asked the question he couldn't answer.

How could this cub be responsible for the death of the Dragon Speaker and the destruction of the Bamboo Kingdom?

Sunset was definitely right about one thing, though, which Ghost had become more and more certain of as he'd spent time playing with Pepper and showing him around: Pepper was hiding something. He would answer questions, but never quite directly. He only talked about his siblings as a unit—never anything like *Shiver said* or *Snowstorm used to*, but always *my siblings*. He would only say he had gotten lost in the dark, and didn't remember where he'd been separated from them or from their mother.

"Come on, it's your turn to chase," Ghost said. "Ready?"

Pepper got to his paws and crouched back. "Ready!"

"Okay . . . *go!*" Ghost sprang into a run, back down the bottom of the little valley and out onto a hillside. He heard Pepper scrambling and laughing behind him, and slowed his pace a little as he turned to climb up a pile of rocks. After all, he had to make sure Pepper was with him.

They chased up and down the hillsides, Ghost leading him farther and farther from the feast clearing and the center of the Prosperhill. At last, Ghost saw ahead the clump of trees he was heading for. With one final pause to look over his shoulder and check that Pepper was still with him, he scrambled up the last of the slope and through the trees to the small, shady clearing, enclosed on all sides but one by tall ferns.

Sunset looked up as he entered. Ghost paused, catching

his breath. They didn't say anything to each other, but Sunset gave Ghost a questioning look, and Ghost nodded. Then he stepped aside so he wouldn't block Pepper's way into the clearing.

Pepper burst into the clearing and skidded to a halt in front of Sunset.

"Caught you!" Sunset chuckled.

Ghost caught the wary look on Pepper's face before it transformed into a happy smile and he sat down, giggling.

"Hello, Dragon Speaker!" Pepper said.

Ghost padded silently behind him and sat down, lounging in the soft moss between the small cub and the way out.

Pepper looked around. "There you are, Ghost! I found you." He walked over and bopped Ghost's nose with his own. Ghost tried to smile.

"Come and sit with me, Pepper," said Sunset.

If Pepper could feel the tension in the air, he didn't show it. He took the bamboo that Sunset nudged toward him, and sat down to eat it, without ever giving another look at Ghost or the gap in the bushes.

"Thank you, Dragon Speaker," he said through a mouthful of bamboo leaves.

"How are you settling in?" Sunset asked, and crunched down on his bamboo cane, splitting it neatly in half.

"Oh, I'm very happy," said Pepper. "I just hope my siblings turn up soon."

Ghost felt, somehow, that Pepper had been wrong to bring

them up so quickly. But he couldn't put his claw on why, exactly.

"Where did you last see them?" Sunset asked. "We've sent out pandas to search, but we've found nothing—it would be much easier if we knew where to start looking."

"In the Northern Forest," said Pepper.

"The Northern Forest is a big place," Sunset chuckled. "What about your mother? What was her name again?"

Ghost knew for certain that Pepper had never named his mother. He paused, chewing and looking up into Sunset's friendly face.

"I just called her Mother," he said.

"And where did you last see her?"

Pepper frowned, scrunching his face up with the effort of remembering. "Um . . . It was when the ground shook. There was a big, tall tree, and a rock that I held on to. . . ."

A tall tree and a rock? He could be talking about absolutely anywhere.

Ghost tried not to stare too intensely at Pepper, but he couldn't figure him out at all. Could he be doing this on purpose? Why would he want them not to find his family? Was it really possible that this young bear already had some plot, some dark ulterior motive for coming here and announcing himself as a triplet, but then giving them no more information?

It didn't make sense.

Sunset obviously thought it didn't make sense either.

"And what about your siblings. What were they called?"

A cheeky glint passed over Pepper's eyes. "I called them

Stinky and Slowpaws," he said, grinning.

"Stinky, Slowpaws, and Pepper," Sunset said evenly. He seemed to seriously consider this for a moment.

Then he bent over, slamming his paw down on to the ground, splintering the bamboo cane under his weight. He brought his face in close to Pepper's, and the mischief drained from Pepper's expression.

"Their. *Real*. Names," he growled.

Now Pepper did glance at Ghost, and Ghost felt his heart squeeze. He wanted to help his new friend. But how could he, if his friend might be plotting against Sunset and the whole kingdom?

Apparently realizing Ghost wouldn't leap to his defense, Pepper seemed to make a decision—but instead of doing the sensible thing and just telling Sunset the other two triplets' names, he forced another cheeky grin, right in the Dragon Speaker's face. "Don't remember," he said.

Is he crazy? Ghost thought. *Why is he behaving like this? It's so obviously suspicious. I'm sure he could have come up with a better lie than that. It's as if he thinks he's already won.*

"You had better remember soon," said Sunset, bringing his muzzle even closer to Pepper's, his voice so low Ghost could feel it rumbling in the pit of his stomach. "Or you will find that the Prosperhill can be much less welcoming." He drew back, and the anger on his face melted back into a practiced, friendly smile. "Ghost will stick close to you. After all, with your terrible memory, anything could happen to you by yourself."

* * *

Ghost watched Pepper as he scampered along the path to say hello to Pebble and Peony, who were sitting together looking out at the river.

He was so *strange*. Ghost had no doubt that he'd understood he was being intimidated, when Sunset had been right in front of him. But he'd seemed to shake it off as soon as they'd left the clearing, and he seemed to bear no ill will toward Ghost, even though he'd been told almost directly that Ghost was working for Sunset and wouldn't let him out of his sight. Pepper knew they didn't trust him or believe his stories, but it didn't seem to dampen his spirits.

What was he planning? And *why*? Possibilities swirled in Ghost's mind, dark thoughts he would really rather not have come up with. Maybe Pepper would steal the blue stone, or smash it? Maybe he'd try to feed Sunset poisoned bamboo, or some other rotten food? Maybe he would trick him into falling into the river or off a cliff?

Whatever Pepper was going to do, Ghost would be there, and he would stop him.

After a while, Pepper yawned hugely and told Ghost he was going to take a nap. Ghost muttered something about that sounding like a good idea, and pretended to yawn too. They both made their way toward the panda nests, and Pepper flopped down happily on the one that Ghost knew belonged to Pebble. In a few moments he was apparently fast asleep. Ghost sat and watched him, amazed that he could relax so completely. Whatever his evil plan, he must be very confident it would work. . . .

"Hey," said a voice, and Ghost looked up to see Shiver making her way across the hillside. Her tail was twitching, and he knew at once that something was bothering her. He smiled, happy to see her after a day spent following Pepper around, but she didn't smile back. She stopped on a rock right above where Pepper was sleeping. "Can I have a word with you?" she hissed. "Not right here?"

Has she heard something about Pepper? Ghost wondered.

"I can't go too far," he whispered.

"Oh yes, I know," said Shiver. Ghost stared at her. Was she . . . angry with him? She stalked a little way away, and Ghost followed her, casting looks back all the time to make sure Pepper was still within sight.

"What's wrong?" he asked, when Shiver stopped and turned.

His sister sat, straight-backed and frowning. Ghost realized that she had grown since they'd arrived at the Prosperhill— she would always be small for a snow leopard, but she'd lost some of her kittenish features. She looked more than ever like a miniature version of Winter.

"I overheard you," she said. "You and Sunset Deepwood. I crept up and listened. You were bullying that cub! Why?"

Ghost was slightly taken aback. But then he sighed, and shook his head.

"I—I guess it could look like that," he said. "If you didn't know what I know."

"Oh yeah?" Shiver asked, giving him a skeptical look. "What did Sunset tell you that makes it seem okay to trick and trap and stalk another panda like that? It isn't like you, Ghost," she added, softening a little.

"It's a secret," Ghost said. He scratched at the ground, frustrated. His secret was so huge, so important. He longed to tell her, but he knew he couldn't—what's more, she didn't believe in the Great Dragon, so what was to say she would even believe in Sunset's prophecy? "There are things happening . . . *important* things, that you don't understand."

Shiver shook her head. "I understand more than you realize. Ghost, Sunset's *using* you."

"What?" Ghost scoffed. "No! That's ridiculous. I do things for him because he's the Dragon Speaker and it's important— and he's my friend! He's been kind to me. He's accepted me when half the pandas here probably wanted to throw me out just for being different."

"And you were desperate to be accepted, right? And Sunset *knew* that." Shiver sighed deeply. "He's been using that to make you do what he wants. I heard him say so."

Ghost's heart was racing. "That's nonsense, and you know it is."

"Oh, is it?" Shiver got to her paws and began to stalk back and forth in front of him, like the tiger on the northern bank. "I suppose I'm a liar, then? I *heard* him, Ghost, talking to Blossom and Horizon and Cypress. He said, 'Ghost's strong and bloodthirsty, but don't worry—he's too stupid to pose a threat'! Those were his *exact* words—they've been running around my head all day!"

Ghost stared at her.

It was impossible. This whole conversation was impossible.

"Why are you saying this? Why are you making it up? I know you don't like it here—are you just jealous, is that it?"

"*Jealous?* Of you and Sunset?" Shiver bared her teeth at him.

"No," Ghost said. It all seemed to fall into place. "Of me finding my place in this world, at last. I was always the one who didn't fit in, when we were growing up. You always had that advantage over me. Now we've come to where *I* belong, and you can't stand it."

"Ghost, you're talking absolute pika droppings," Shiver snarled. "Stop it."

"No, I won't. I like it here. I've got real friends now. But you've been complaining ever since we arrived. All you do is think about how much better it'd be if we still lived in the White Spine and followed the Snow Cat. If it's so terrible here, why don't you go back?"

Shiver yowled, her fur fluffing up along the back of her neck as if she were facing down a rival leopard. "Maybe I should! You're right. This is no place for a snow leopard, and if you'd rather believe that liar over your own sister, maybe you *do* belong here. I'm going home. You can come find me when your precious Dragon Speaker finally betrays you."

And with that she stalked past him, brushing her shoulder against his, and broke into a run.

Wait.... The word rose up in Ghost's throat, and then died as Shiver slipped between the trees and was gone, leaving him alone.

Ghost snuck up to the edge of the river and peered across. He sniffed at the air.

"I think it's gone," he said. Sunset stepped up behind him.

"Good," he said. "A tiger is an inconvenience we do not need today."

His calm voice betrayed no hint of the fear Ghost had seen in him when they had sighted the tiger on the opposite bank. Ghost couldn't blame him for covering it. It definitely didn't make him a liar.

Shiver's words had lain heavy on his shoulders all day. He was certain she was wrong, that she'd heard some other panda talking about him—probably Blossom—or that she'd made it up out of jealousy just to get at him.

He missed her already, even though he tried not to think about her.

Pepper hadn't done anything for the rest of the day but eat, sleep, play with the oblivious Prosperhill cubs, and continue to spin stories about his siblings that were possibly true but infuriatingly vague. Sunset had left Pebble in charge of him while he and Ghost crossed the river to join the search for more missing pandas, hoping to find Pepper's siblings even without his help. Ghost worried about Sunset's choice. Pebble was nice . . . maybe a bit too nice.

He tried to focus on where he was putting his paws as he led the way out past the Egg Rocks, onto the river path. It was a little wider and shallower now, the river settling back even further into its old path.

Shiver probably crossed here already, he thought as he splashed through the cold water and up onto the northern bank.

Now that he'd spent so much time in the Prosperhill, it was strange to Ghost that he had ever found the Northern Forest overwhelmingly green and lush. As soon as they left the edge of the river, the hills started to look more bare. They saw the occasional clump of bamboo canes, but nothing like the forests of it that grew on the other side of the river. The trees here tended to be tall and thin, and the moss underpaw was wet but not as springy.

They made their way upriver first, climbing a steep hillside, scenting all the time for traces of young pandas. Ghost supposed he would know the missing two triplets, if he saw them—he guessed they would look just like Pepper.

They stopped at the top, and Sunset looked out over the Northern Forest, his muzzle twitching.

"They'll be on their way to us," he said. "They'll want to be reunited with their brother. I would much prefer for us to find them first. Then they won't have time to compare their stories."

Ghost nodded slowly.

"Sunset . . . do you think it's already too late for Pepper? I mean, do you think the Dragon warned you about the triplets in time to persuade them not to turn bad?"

"Going by Pepper's behavior? I worry it may already be too late," Sunset said. "But I hope not."

They traveled for the rest of Long Light and Sun Fall, sweeping a wide path first upriver and then downriver from the Egg Rocks. They celebrated the Feast of Sun Fall together, alone on a hillside covered in brown ferns, and Ghost felt both very privileged and slightly awkward to be receiving the blessing from the Dragon Speaker, all by himself.

They scented panda trails as they walked on, but they were old and faint, and Ghost began to think that the other triplets had gone another way, or were hiding somewhere much farther afield.

The last rays of the sun were slanting through the trees, casting bright shafts of light and deep dark shadows, when they caught a much fresher scent. Sunset's ears pricked up and he let Ghost lead the way, sniffing through the undergrowth until he stepped out into a thin gingko forest carpeted with faded yellow leaves.

There was a panda sitting there, a bamboo cane clutched in her paws. She turned to look at them, and Ghost felt a jolt of recognition, and then dismay.

The panda was a female, too old to be one of the triplets, and she had a long claw-mark scar across her muzzle. She was looking at him with the same wide eyes of recognition turning to horror.

That scar had been made by his claws. It was the panda he

had attacked in the mountain cave.

She sprang to her feet and backed away, growling.

"Wait, please," he said. "I'm—"

He wanted to say he was sorry, that he'd thought she was trying to attack him in the dark, that he was glad to see she was alive. But the female's gaze had flickered over his shoulder to where Sunset was emerging from the forest behind him.

"You . . . ," she muttered, cutting Ghost off. "I know you. *Sunset Deepwood.*" She stopped backing away, and instead stepped forward, baring her teeth. "So, the white monster is yours, is it? I should have known. A false Dragon Speaker who lost his powers and turned to violence. Well, it won't do you any good to kill me now."

Ghost glanced at Sunset. What was this panda talking about?

"Plum Risingtree," said Sunset, with a chill in his voice. "I remember you too. And I'm afraid you're making a mistake."

"Oh? And what's my mistake? Are you *not* a fraud, Sunset? Did you not send this bear to the mountains to look for my sister's cubs? You're a wicked pair of liars, that's clear."

"I wasn't looking for anyone in the mountains," Ghost put in. "I don't know what you're talking about, nor does Sunset. And he hasn't lost his powers!"

Plum just shook her head at Sunset, circling him, her muzzle curling up around the scar tissue. "You may think you've already disposed of one, but I tell you now, all three of Orchid's triplets live."

Ghost couldn't help gasping, and looking at Sunset again. Sunset's eyes were wide and fixed on Plum's face, as if he couldn't quite believe what she was saying either.

"Shadowhunter has found two already. They know their destinies, and they're coming for you. I will help them expose you for the liar you are, and they will rule as Dragon Speakers long after you are dead!"

With that, Plum threw herself across the clearing, right at Sunset.

Sunset gave a mighty roar and surged forward to meet her. Ghost hardly had time to react before the two of them were violently grappling, scratching and biting. Plum sank her teeth into Sunset's shoulder and he yelped in pain, his legs weakening beneath him. She drove him to the ground. But Sunset roared and pushed back, reaching up and clawing at her sides, leaving deep bloody scratches along her ribs.

How can this be happening? There was blood and fur spattered across the ground. The Dragon Speaker was biting down on Plum's leg. Plum had one paw pressed against his face, trying to shove him away.

Ghost felt as if he were wading through rushing water as he ran toward them. He put his head down and butted into Plum's shoulder with all his might. She lost her grip on Sunset and tumbled, rolling onto her back.

"Get away from the Dragon Speaker!" Ghost yelled. "Get back!"

She scrambled to her paws, holding the one Sunset had

wounded up off the ground.

"You'll pay for it all," she hissed.

Sunset opened his mouth and let out a roar that seemed to shake the leaves of the gingko trees. Then he charged again, and Ghost ran by his side. But Plum clearly knew she was beaten. She turned and scrambled away into the trees, limping and leaving a trail of blood and fur behind.

Sunset stopped at the edge of the clearing and watched her go.

"You're hurt," Ghost said, staring at the bite wound on the Dragon Speaker's shoulder.

"I'm all right. I've survived worse," said Sunset. He glared after Plum for another few moments, anger seething in his eyes. Then he looked back at Ghost and sagged, turning his eyes to the ground. The fury in his face was quickly replaced by pity. "That . . . that poor panda. I did know her, before the flood. She wasn't always like this." He turned to Ghost. "Is it true that you gave her that scar, in the mountains?"

Ghost nodded miserably. "I didn't mean to! It was dark in the cave, and I had never seen a panda before, and she came rushing at me. . . ." He trailed off. It didn't sound all that convincing, even to him, though it was the truth. What would Pebble say, when he found out? Would the Prosperhill pandas reject him once and for all?

Sunset raised his front paw, on the side that hadn't been bitten, and placed it on Ghost's shoulder. "You don't have to make excuses to me. I believe you. But I think that explains this . . . this madness. The wound probably went bad, and the sickness has addled her mind."

"No . . . ," Ghost groaned, feeling dizzy, as if the ground under his paws were shifting. "*I* did this to her? I—I was just scared. I didn't mean for anything like this to happen!"

Sunset sighed. "Don't worry. I know it wasn't your fault. And I won't tell the others. In fact, I think this whole unfortunate incident is probably best left between you and me. Some of the Prosperhill pandas were her friends once. They don't need to know the state she's in now."

Ghost nodded, panting with relief. Sunset was such a good friend. As for what she had said about the triplets . . . He guessed he and Sunset could discuss that another time.

"Let's go home," Sunset said. "Yet again, I'm glad you were here with me, Ghost."

A little burst of pride overcame the guilt in Ghost's heart and warmed him in the chill evening air. "You can lean on me if you need to, as we walk," he said, placing himself on Sunset's left, uninjured side.

"Thank you," said Sunset. "I don't know what I'd do without you."

CHAPTER SIXTEEN

RAIN LAY FLAT, BREATHING slowly, behind a wall of shifting green bamboo canes.

She was waiting. She had been waiting for two days, from Gray Light to Moon Fall. She had crept closer and closer to the center of the Prosperhill until she'd found a vantage point where she could see but not be seen, a small flat rock that was near the hill where the pandas made their nests but shielded from sight by a thick screen of bamboo. Then she had waited, not stirring a hair except in the deep, dark part of the night when she was confident that none of the Prosperhill pandas would hear her sneak upright and rustle the bamboo enough to feed on the soft leaves. Even then, she had resisted the urge to snap down any of the canes, or stray too far from her hiding place.

She napped occasionally, but mostly she watched. She saw

pandas come and go, in ones and twos, and at the end of the day almost all of them arrived together, resting in their hollows or on the low branches of trees. She was too far away to hear anything that was said, but she noticed several pandas she had never met before—more results of Sunset's drive to gather pandas to him, presumably. There was the strange white one and the small one, the two who were clearly mates, and some others.

It had been painful sometimes. She'd seen Sunset, and not only had to not growl at him, but had to watch as her friends and family treated him like the Dragon Speaker he was pretending to be. She had watched Pebble and Peony, her heart aching as she noticed that more often than not they stuck together.

She was waiting for her moment, and it finally came. The area around her rock was deserted, but coming slowly up the panda path toward her was Peony. She was alone, at last.

It was the hardest thing Rain had had to do since she'd first suspected Sunset, but she forced herself to wait even longer, just a few more seconds, until she was completely sure that no other pandas were following Peony or close enough to hear her and come running.

Then she scrambled down from her rock, dropped into a pile of leaves, and bowled out onto the path, only a single bear-length from her mother.

Peony stumbled, her legs wobbling.

"Rain!" she choked. "How . . ." Then she rushed forward

and barreled into Rain, hitting her so hard that Rain staggered, and covered her face and neck in licks and nuzzling. "My baby! My sweet cub!"

"Shh, shh, I'm here," said Rain, returning the nuzzles. "I'm back, it's okay."

"You're alive!" Peony pulled away from Rain so she could stare into her face, as if to check it was really her. "How? Sunset saw you drown!"

Rain nuzzled her mother again. Now that it came to it, she almost wanted to put off the next thing she needed to say, because she knew that it would hurt Peony to hear it.

"Sunset *said* he saw me drown," she said. "But here I am. Mother, Sunset Deepwood is a liar."

Peony stared at her, the joy of disbelief turning to pure confusion. Rain hung her head.

"Can we get off the path? We need to talk."

"It seems like we do," Peony muttered. "Come on. I know a place."

The hollow where Peony led her was such a good hiding place, Rain wished she'd found it herself. It was a small dip in the ground at the base of a tall tree, completely surrounded and covered by tall ferns. Rain and Peony pushed through the ferns and lay down together in the soft green space, curling up as close as they could, Rain's head laid across Peony's paws, Peony's chin resting on the top of Rain's head, just like they had when Rain was a little cub.

"Tell me everything," Peony said.

It all came out in a rush. Her suspicions about Sunset, the monkeys, Maple, the striped bamboo. The confrontation by the river, the fake prophecy he'd tried to use to get her on his side, and then the attack. As she described Sunset holding her head underwater, she could feel her mother's chest vibrating with a growl, her paws tensed with shock and anger.

"I'll kill him," Peony said. "How dare he lay a paw on you? And then to tell us all you'd—I should have known. I should never have believed that you would have drowned by accident."

"It's not your fault," Rain told her. "He's got them all fooled. They all think he's the true Dragon Speaker."

"Let's go," said Peony, starting to get up. "We have to tell the others!"

"Not yet." Rain put a paw over her mother's. "I should tell you the rest. Something really strange happened to me on the other side of the river."

Peony sat back, her head tilted curiously.

"I was pulled out of the water by another panda," Rain said. "A female, my age, with the same white grip pad I have. She said we were sisters. And I told her that was insane, but she wasn't done yet. She took me up into the mountains. I met an older panda, called Plum, and there was a *tiger* with them, and he told me that she and I were two out of a litter of triplet cubs, and that the three of us were the children of some panda called Orchid and destined to . . . to be *Dragon Speakers. . . .*"

Rain paused, her heart turning over in her chest at the sight of Peony's expression. Her mother was looking up at her with recognition and dawning awe in her eyes.

"And I told them it was all nonsense," Rain went on, but there was a questioning tone in her voice now. "Or maybe it's not, maybe Leaf really is the Dragon Speaker—I could believe that—but I told them, I *have* a mother . . . her name's Peony. . . ."

She fell silent. Peony looked like she could hardly breathe. She sat up straight, pulling away from Rain, clearly trying to gather her thoughts.

"Just tell me," Rain whispered. "Tell me everything."

"Rain . . . you are my cub, and I love you. You will always be my cub. But . . ." She shook her head. "I didn't give birth to you."

Rain had known, as soon as she'd seen Peony's reaction to the name Orchid, but now, hearing it said out loud, she felt like some huge paw had lifted up her whole life and tipped it upside down.

"Your real mother was called Orchid," Peony went on. "The tiger was right about that. She was my best friend. She lived here, in the Southern Forest, before the flood. You were born right in the middle of it, she told me. Her mate, Root— your father—was attacked by a troop of monkeys and fell into the river, and she had to give birth to you, all alone, in the worst storm the Bamboo Kingdom had ever seen."

"She wasn't completely alone," Rain murmured, almost to herself. "Shadowhunter the tiger found her."

"When she brought you to me, after the storm had died down, she told me she'd had twins, and that you were both in terrible danger. She said she had to go far away to hide her other cub, and asked me to take care of you and raise you as my own?"

"Twins?" Rain muttered. "She didn't mention a third?"

"No," said Peony. "But if it's true, if you are . . . Well, I can see why she would want to keep that a secret, even from me. I—I always thought that the trauma of it all, the birth, losing Root, it had just gotten too much for her. I never thought that when she said you were in danger, she could mean that . . ."

"That I would be . . . a Dragon Speaker," said Rain. She felt dizzy, as if she were back in the river being buffeted this way and that by the cold currents.

Peony trod the ground in front of her nervously. "Rain, I am *so* sorry. I was going to tell you, someday. I love you so much—can you ever forgive me?"

Rain stared at her.

I ought to be angry, she thought. *You lied to me. I ran from my sister—my real twin sister—because I believed your lie.*

But there was no anger in her heart. She thought of her earliest memories, of snuggling up to Peony on cold or rainy nights, of trailing after her on her way to the feast clearing, of Peony telling her to be patient or be nice, Peony teaching her to swim, Peony defending her when she was in trouble.

"I forgive you," she said. "Of course I do! You're my mother, no matter what. I love you." She stepped forward and pressed her forehead to Peony's. Peony let out a strangled laugh and nuzzled against her.

"I am your mother," she said. "And whatever you want to do next—about Sunset, about any of it—I'll be right by your side. You're my daughter . . . and my Dragon Speaker."

It was Rain's turn to give a tense and croaking laugh. "I can't believe—I mean, *why*?" she said. "Leaf is real Dragon Speaker material, a true believer; she wouldn't be swayed from what she thought her duty to the Dragon was, no matter what I said or did. But me . . . I'm . . . not like that. I didn't even believe I'd *seen* the Dragon until . . . well, kind of until right now," she said. She thought of the vision in the mist from the waterfall—a dragon with three heads. She thought of the bones in the river, which she'd *seen* while she should have been drowning. She thought of the curling black *something* that had pulled her out of Sunset's grip and farther into the water. "I'm stubborn, and kind of selfish, and I don't do what I'm told. Why would the Dragon choose me?"

She realized Peony was looking at her with a familiar, and very slightly infuriating, look of pure affection on her face.

"You're going to be a wonderful Dragon Speaker," she said. "Trust me."

Rain rolled her eyes. "You have to say that," she said. "You're my mother." But all the same, she felt as if the world had, at last, stopped spinning.

Rain watched through her screen of bamboo as Sunset walked up the path.

He wasn't alone. He was almost never alone, not as far as she could make out. Peony had helped her find hiding places and travel between them, and so far she hadn't caught Sunset by himself even once—either he was followed by a gaggle of adoring pandas asking him questions and bringing him news and gifts, or he was meeting with the golden monkeys, or he was flanked by Blossom and Ginseng, who seemed to have fallen into the role of guards or advisers . . . or he was walking with the white panda.

It was the two of them now, walking up the path past the nesting hill. As they passed, she knew she ought to be watching Sunset, but she couldn't seem to take her eyes off the white panda. He was so strange to look at, more muscular and less fluffy than many of the others, and he moved differently too. More like a cat than a bear.

She remembered what Plum had said about her attacker in the mountain cave. *The white monster.* Rain had assumed it must be a mountain leopard—or a figment of Plum's imagination—but what if she was wrong? A lot of other things she'd assumed had turned out to be wrong. What if Sunset had sent him into the mountains looking for Leaf?

She watched them both retreating up the hill, and sagged.

I don't know what to do, she thought. *Now that I'm here, I don't know the best way to get rid of Sunset.*

She'd always known that he had most of the Prosperhill pandas in his thrall, but it seemed worse now than when she'd left. Even if she marched up to the feast clearing, even though he'd told them she was dead, she was afraid they wouldn't believe he was a liar.

She could almost hear Leaf's voice in her head. *Is it possible that you should have had a bit more of a plan before coming back here? Maybe some backup?*

She mentally swatted at her imaginary sister.

I'm here now. I'll find a way. I just need a little . . . guidance.

She sat up and stretched, listening intently for the sounds of nearby pandas. There was one thing she hadn't tried, one source of guidance she hadn't yet directly asked.

If she really was a Dragon Speaker, the Great Dragon would want her to succeed.

It took her a little longer to find the waterfall than she expected. She remembered where it should be, but everything had changed so much since the river had receded. The rocks that had formed the waterfall now jutted out of the bank, dry and jagged. Instead of a deep, churning pool, the rocks now surrounded a shallow circle of clear, still water that was partially separate from the flow of the river. Rain could walk right up to it across the silty mud bank.

The Dragon's always come to me by the river, she thought. *I don't know why, but I'm sure I'm still in the right place.*

She sat down beside the shallows and let the water lap over her paws. The familiarity of it was calming.

All right, Great Dragon, she thought. *I'm here. I believe. Please help me. . . .*

There was no waterfall now to look into, so presumably her answer wouldn't come in the form of mist. Instead she stared at the pool and tried to relax, focusing on the way the light shone through the leaves of trees far overhead and shimmered on the clear surface of the pool. It was so calm she could see her own reflection looking back at her, just as she had when Sunset had tried to convince her he was showing her a vision. . . .

The pool darkened. For a moment Rain thought it was just the sun passing behind a cloud, and perhaps that was happening too. But the colors in the pool shifted from green and brown to gray and then almost to black. Her reflection was still and clear.

And then, over the reflection's shoulder, another panda face slowly crept into view.

It was . . . *also her.* But the eyes were different. They were wrong.

The Rain behind her reared back, raised its paws, and shoved her into the water.

Rain yelled and flailed, spinning around ready to fight, but there was nothing there. It was only after a moment's breathless staring into the trees that she realized that she hadn't felt any paws on her back either.

It was a vision.

She looked back into the pool, but it was clear, its colors bright, and her reflection faint and broken from where her scrambling had disturbed the surface.

A panda with my face . . . but it wasn't me.

Some panda pretending to be her? Who wanted to take her place, get her out of the way?

"Well . . . yeah," she murmured out loud. "Sunset's pretending to be a Dragon Speaker. He tried to drown me. That happened already." She stared back into the pool. Her reflection was coming back together, but no matter how hard she glared at it, it seemed that was all the vision she was getting. "Listen," she grumbled. "I'm trying. You sent me a vision! I believe; it's amazing. But I was really hoping you'd be a bit more helpful than that! I *know* Sunset's a fraud—the part I need help with is *stopping* him."

There was no answer from the pool.

Rain sighed.

She would just have to do this herself.

CHAPTER SEVENTEEN

SUNSET SAT ON HIS rock, his eyes closed and his nose tipped toward the sky. He passed the blue stone from paw to paw, almost restlessly. Ghost watched with a sense of anxiety building in his chest. What was the Dragon saying to him? Would it be something about Pepper?

The rest of the pandas stared up silently at their Dragon Speaker, and Ghost wondered if they had noticed Sunset's agitation too. The longer Sunset's eyes stayed closed, the more he passed the stone back and forth and back and forth, the more the tension in the air of the feast clearing grew.

Could he be having trouble? Ghost wondered. *The monkeys brought him that striped bamboo, and he hasn't eaten any at this feast. Does it help him hear the Dragon's voice?*

Finally Sunset let out a huge sigh, his shoulders rising and then sagging. He wobbled slightly on his rock and let his chin fall, his eyes blinking open. He stared ahead for a moment, still not speaking. Ghost could feel the breathing of the pandas next to him hitch as without a word he got down from the rock and stood among them, in the very center of the clearing.

For a moment longer, he still didn't speak. He seemed to be gathering himself.

"My friends," he said finally, "the Great Dragon has sent me a difficult message. The Dragon itself is worried about us. We are in danger."

A shudder seemed to run around the clearing, stirring the fur of every panda who heard Sunset's warning. No panda spoke, but Ghost could feel them pressing forward, desperate to know what kind of danger awaited them. He dug his claws into the ground and watched Sunset with a firm stare. Whatever it was, he would be ready for it.

"The Dragon tells me there is a liar in the forest," Sunset went on. "They plan to do us harm. We must all be vigilant."

Is it Pepper? Ghost wondered.

"Funny how the Dragon never tells you names," said a voice. Ghost spun around and looked up to see Brawnshanks sprawled in the branch of a tree, his tail and one leg swinging. All around him, a crowd of golden monkeys sat watching the pandas, or looking bored and scratching themselves. Ghost's muzzle twitched in a silent growl. It bothered him that the monkeys could creep up to the heart of the Prosperhill without being heard, if it suited them.

"If *I* were a Great Dragon," Brawnshanks went on, "I'd be specific. Tell you exactly who to watch out for."

"It doesn't work like that," elderly Mist retorted, glaring up at Brawnshanks. "Disrespectful monkey."

"He's kind of got a point," said Goby. Several of the other pandas turned to look at him in disapproval, but some of the younger ones nodded. "Can't the Great Dragon tell you more about who to look out for? Didn't it give you *any* clues?"

All heads in the clearing turned to Sunset, and for a moment, Ghost saw a flicker of anger crease the fur between his eyes. Then he shook his head sadly.

"I'm afraid the visions don't come to me that way," he said with a kind smile at Goby. "Only a Dragon Speaker can ever experience them, so I understand that it may seem strange. But it's not for us to question the Dragon's wisdom, only to follow its advice—if we do not, we risk damaging the balance of the kingdom once again."

"The flood," whispered Lily to Crag, just behind Ghost, and this thought echoed through the rest of the assembled pandas. Goby nodded sadly.

"My honorable friend Brawnshanks," Sunset said, taking a step toward the tree where the golden monkeys were roosting like hefty, restless birds. "I know that your kind struggles to understand the will of the Dragon, and you have my sympathies. But I suggest that if you cannot listen quietly and try to understand, you leave this clearing."

Brawnshanks stretched, then pulled both feet up onto the

branch so he was squatting, looking down at Sunset with his front paws on his back knees.

"I'm just saying," he chortled, "the Bamboo Kingdom is full of liars, cheats, and frauds—isn't it, Dragon Speaker? One more won't make much difference, will it?"

He leaped away without waiting for Sunset's reply, and the golden monkeys followed his lead with a chattering whoop of laughter, vanishing back into the forest with none of the stealth they'd used to approach.

"I bet it's him," Ghost heard Frog whisper to Fir.

"We can only pity those poor creatures who don't know how to follow the Dragon's wisdom," Sunset said, though Ghost noticed he was saying it through gritted teeth. "And show them the way whenever we can."

And with that, he turned on the spot and walked away. The pandas began to disperse, most of them cheerful enough. But Ghost knew Sunset well enough by now to notice that his muscles were tense as he walked, his claws spiking into the earth with every step.

It must be hard to be the Speaker and deal with creatures like Brawnshanks, he thought as he watched Sunset go. *But I hope he doesn't let the monkey distract him. Whether it's Pepper or someone else who's the liar, we all need to be vigilant—including him.*

Ghost stepped into the river, glancing both ways along the bank in case he spotted the tiger again, but there was no sign of it.

He'd figured out how he could best help Sunset. The Dragon Speaker didn't seem to want to talk to anyone right now—perhaps the vision had disturbed him even more than it seemed. But he'd said they needed to be vigilant, and with Pepper happily collecting bamboo under the observation of Ginseng and Pebble, the most vigilant thing he could think to do was go back to the Northern Forest and try again to find the other two triplets. Maybe Pepper was the liar, or one of the others would be, or it could be something else entirely. Whatever the truth, he knew he would feel better for putting his knowledge of the situation to use, rather than lying around pretending that everything was normal.

Sure enough, he'd barely gone a few bear-lengths into the Northern Forest when he sensed that something was wrong. He heard raised voices downriver. He hurried in their direction, anxiety gripping his heart tighter and tighter as he grew closer.

A high wail of distress split the air. Ghost broke into a run, pounding along the muddy bank until he came around a bend, his paws slipping, and saw a small group of pandas gathered around something at the edge of the water.

Two of them were Bay and Azalea Prosperhill, who must have been exploring the northern bank too. There was also a panda he didn't know—it was this one who had let out the horrible cry. She was crouched low, poking at the thing floating in the water and keening to herself.

Dread seemed to rise from the mud and cling to Ghost's

fur, making it hard to step forward and look closer at what was in the water. But he forced himself to confirm his awful suspicions.

Sure enough, the river streamed red from the spot where the pandas stood, and as he came closer he could see a black paw, and a white muzzle . . . a muzzle with a long and jagged scar over it.

"No, *Plum*," moaned the unknown panda. "How could this happen to you?"

Azalea looked around, saw Ghost, and sighed, bowing her head. "Something's killed one of the Northern Forest pandas," she explained sadly.

Ghost nodded and stepped closer, but he felt as if he were floating away from his own body as he did so.

"I don't understand," said the Northern Forest panda. Her voice sounded dim and strange to Ghost. "The last we heard she was with her niece. They were making their way to the Darkpool. How did this happen?"

"It looks like she's had a tough time," said Bay softly, indicating the scars. Ghost felt sick.

"I'm going to get the Dragon Speaker," Azalea said, and hurried past Ghost, back upriver toward the Egg Rocks.

The Northern Forest panda looked up, her grief-filled face turning to surprise.

"What's your name?" Bay asked her.

"Grass Darkpool," whispered the panda. She was still staring after Azalea. Then she shook herself and looked back at

Plum, sadness clouding her gaze again. "This was Plum. She was my friend, back when we were both Slenderwoods."

Ghost forced himself to look at the body. It was covered in scratches and bites, deep welts that looked painful as well as fatal. It hadn't been an easy death, or a quick one.

"She was a kind, good panda," said Grass. "She left us to climb the White Spine Mountains, to look for answers about . . . about the flood. We heard she was on her way back. She wasn't supposed to be alone. . . ."

She was alone by the time we met her in the forest, Ghost thought. He chewed lightly on his tongue, just to make absolutely certain he wouldn't accidentally say it out loud. It should be Sunset's decision whether they told the others about their encounter.

They stayed together by the body for a little while longer, and then Ghost heard paw steps on the mud behind him, and he turned to see Sunset and Azalea, with Peony and Blossom following behind them.

Sunset slowed his pace as he approached Plum's body, and bent his head close to hers with a sigh of deep sadness.

"I knew Plum a little before the flood," he told Grass and Bay. "I'm so very sorry her life ended this way." He reached out and gently moved one of Plum's sodden paws, inspecting the scratches and bite marks. "I'm afraid I know what must have happened—poor Plum ran afoul of the tiger that's been spotted hunting near the river."

Bay gasped, and Blossom shook her head.

Ghost looked again at the wounds.

Could that be right . . . ?

"Predators," Blossom spat, with a glance at Ghost, which Ghost tried to ignore.

"Quiet," Peony admonished her.

Sunset laid a paw gently on Plum's forehead. "Great Dragon, please guide Plum's spirit to the mountain in the sky," he said, in a deep voice. "Now we must return and break the sad news to the others. Grass," he added, looking at the Darkpool panda, "will you join us in the Prosperhill? There is as much bamboo as you could want, and many pandas who would love to meet you and hear all about poor Plum."

Grass hesitated for a long moment, looking at Sunset. Ghost wasn't sure why, but he thought a look of outright hostility crossed her face before she bowed to him and backed away. "I have pandas of my own, waiting for me," she said, and vanished into the trees before Sunset could say anything else.

"Very well." Sunset motioned for the other pandas to join him, and set off back toward the river crossing.

Ghost let them get ahead of him, padding slowly and then stopping. He would catch up. But he needed a minute to himself.

He waited until they had gone around the bend and disappeared before he went back to the body. He knew that he couldn't explain to them what he was doing. He wasn't even quite sure of it himself. Gently, with guilt and sadness heavy on his shoulders, he pushed Plum over in the water, once and then again, checking her wounds. It was just as he'd thought—the wounds were deep, but they were almost random, as if they'd been sustained in a drawn-out fight with an attacker. She had probably bled out, or perhaps died from shock or from a blow to the head.

That's not how a predator would kill its prey, Ghost thought. Even if it had no intention of eating her, surely a tiger would finish a fight like this quickly, with a bite to the back of the neck, just like he used to do when the cubs Born of Winter hunted rabbits in the mountains. Why draw it out and risk the creature landing a last desperate blow that could give you a limp or a blind eye and make it hard to feed yourself in the future?

He couldn't know for certain, of course, but if they had asked Ghost, he wouldn't ever have said Plum was killed by a tiger.

It was odd that Sunset could be so mistaken. But he had probably been shaken by seeing her again too. . . .

"Ghost!" Sunset barked. Ghost spun around, kicking up river droplets, and saw Sunset standing by the bend in the bank, watching him. "Come on, we have work to do."

Ghost hurried to Sunset's side, feeling embarrassed. He wondered if he should mention his observations to the Dragon Speaker, but something about Sunset's manner told him it wasn't the right time.

Ghost could see Peony, Blossom, Azalea, and Bay as they rounded the bend, but they were quite some way ahead, and Sunset didn't hurry to catch up with them.

"Plum is dead," he said suddenly. "A tragedy, to be certain.

But it does mean she can no longer spread her crazy ideas to the Prosperhill, and for that I thank the Great Dragon. There is, however, one more panda who can still turn the kingdom against us. I think it's time we dealt with Pepper."

Sunset's words made Ghost's fur prickle and stand on end. What was Sunset planning?

They didn't speak all the way back to the feast clearing. Sunset gave a short explanation of what had happened, and he comforted the pandas who had known Plum before the flood, but his words were quick and perfunctory. All the time, it seemed like he had something else he would rather be doing, and sure enough, as soon as he'd delivered the news, he turned to Pepper and told him to follow him.

It wasn't a request, and Ghost immediately fell back into his role as a guard, even though Pepper went willingly. He still seemed mostly oblivious to the trouble he might be in, or else very good at pretending not to notice Sunset's dark mood.

Sunset led them a little way away from the feast clearing, although they didn't go as far as the circle of trees—Sunset didn't seem to have the patience to go that far. They found a secluded clearing, and Sunset immediately turned on Pepper.

"Where are your siblings?" he growled.

"I don't know," Pepper said, yet again.

"Describe them!"

"They're pandas," said Pepper, almost as if he couldn't stop himself making the silly joke, even though he knew Sunset was in no mood to hear it.

"I was warned about a liar coming to the Prosperhill," Sunset said. He stalked close to Pepper, his nose almost pressed to the young bear's. The way that he moved made Ghost's paws tingle. He looked like a predator. It almost made Ghost step forward and put himself between them, though he wasn't sure if it was Sunset or Pepper he wanted to protect. "Are you that liar, Pepper? I'm starting to think so," Sunset asked.

"What if you're the liar?" said Pepper.

There was a long, awful silence. Sunset almost seemed to swell in size as he stared down at Pepper, his flanks heaving with every furious breath.

Ghost felt as if he were standing at the top of a steep hill, unbalanced, about to fall.

"Maybe you're a triplet; maybe you're not," Sunset said. "Either way, we can't trust you. And we don't need you anymore."

And he lashed out, claws raking through the air toward Pepper's throat.

Ghost was too slow to react, shock thumping through him like the first roaring tremor of an earthquake.

But Pepper was fast, and he was ready. He dropped to the ground and rolled away. Sunset roared and lunged forward to try to seize the small panda between his jaws, and his teeth did scrape Pepper's shoulder, drawing a trickle of blood, but Pepper managed to wiggle free with a cry of terror and scramble to his paws. Sunset tried to swipe at him once more, but Pepper was gone into the bushes, squeezing through a gap where no panda Sunset's size could follow.

"You won't escape!" Sunset roared.

Ghost just stared.

Sunset had tried to kill Pepper. To tear him apart, right in front of Ghost.

"Ghost!" Sunset snapped, and Ghost realized it wasn't the first time he'd called his name. "I need you to focus now. You know what you have to do. Become the white monster. Save the Bamboo Kingdom from this lying, traitorous cub."

For another moment, Ghost still just stared at him. *Become the white monster?*

"Go after him," Sunset said, his voice a low growl that seemed to shake the ground below him. "And make sure he *never* returns to the Southern Forest. Do I make myself clear?"

"Yes," Ghost whispered.

He turned and stumbled away into the undergrowth.

You've made yourself very, very clear.

CHAPTER EIGHTEEN

"ARE YOU SURE ABOUT this?" Peony whispered. "If you want, we could leave now. Just the two of us. We could go and find those Darkpool pandas, and your sister."

Rain swallowed hard. She peered through the ferns, watching the panda path.

"I can't," she said. "I have to try to stop him. What about the rest of the Prosperhill? What about Pebble? This is the only plan I could come up with, so this is what I'm going to do. If he knows his lies are about to be exposed, maybe he'll take the opportunity to save his own skin. He'd hate to be humiliated, I'm sure of it."

So now they were waiting for Sunset to come back. Rain had been watching the pandas come and go since Sunset had returned with Bay and Azalea and the news of what happened to Plum.

More lies. Rain didn't know what had really killed Plum, but she could guess. There was certainly no way Shadowhunter was responsible. Peony had been too upset to describe it clearly, and Rain was almost glad. She felt a terrible numbness when she thought about Plum, and about how Leaf would feel when she heard the news.

If I'd stayed with her, would she have lived? Or would I have died?

She would never know the answer to those questions.

Sunset had set off into the forest with the white panda and the new one at his heels, and none of them had yet returned.

Peony nuzzled gently against Rain's cheek, and Rain could feel that she was trembling slightly. "This is a very brave thing you're doing," she said. "No matter what happens, remember that I'm proud of you."

"I know," said Rain, and nuzzled her too, before returning her attention to the path.

Several pandas wandered past, in pairs or in small groups—no panda seemed to want to walk alone right now.

Except . . .

Finally, here came Sunset. He was by himself—no adoring pandas, no guards, and no monkeys. He trudged up the path slowly, his hackles raised and his gaze fixed on the ground in front of him. He looked preoccupied. Rain wasn't sure if he was anxious or angry.

Peony gave Rain a small nod and slipped away from her, hurrying around to a position behind Sunset. After a moment, there was a loud crack as she bit into a branch. Sunset looked around, and while he was distracted, Rain stepped out of the ferns and onto the path.

Sunset turned back and saw Rain, and his jaw went satisfyingly slack.

"You," he breathed. "You're . . . you can't be back. You drowned. You're dead!"

For a moment Rain didn't even speak; she just stood there and enjoyed his dismay.

"You drowned me, you mean," she said. "And no, I'm not dead. The river saved me. And now I'm back to tell everyone all about you. You've lost your powers. You've made a deal with the monkeys for that striped bamboo you think nobody knows about. You've been bringing pandas here for your own twisted reasons. And you tried to murder me. You're a liar and a fraud, and you're no Dragon Speaker."

It felt so good to get it all out, right to his face, but Rain was irritated to notice that his eyes had come unfocused. The list of his crimes seemed to wash over him, as if his attention was elsewhere.

"The river *saved* you," he said. "Of course. I should have known what you were! Under my nose all along. A triplet."

Rain sniffed, trying not to look surprised. Of course he knew about them.

"Where are the other two?" Sunset snarled, stepping forward. "What about your mother?"

"Her mother's right here," said Peony, stepping out of the bushes behind him.

Sunset spun to face her. "How long have you known your cub was one of the prophecy triplets? Where are her siblings? What are their names?" He started to advance on Peony, who suddenly looked afraid. Anger flared in Rain's chest.

"Hey!" she yelled, starting to back away up the path. "She didn't know any of it. It's me you need to worry about— and I'm off to tell the whole Prosperhill about what you've done!"

Sunset wheeled around. His eyes fixed on Rain. Fear sprouted alongside the anger in her heart, but she kept backing away, slowly, feeling for the path with her back paws.

"Oh yes?" he growled. "You want to tell the pandas everything? Let me *help* you."

He sprang forward. Rain turned, her paws kicking up mud and fallen leaves, and started to run up the path to the feast clearing. She leaped over a rock and scrambled up a hill, hearing the pounding of Sunset's paws right behind her, and Peony's behind his. She had to make it to the clearing before he could stop her. It wasn't far—she could make it, she was sure she could.

She took a shortcut up a steep bank and through a patch of ferns, but he was right on her tail, and as they burst out onto the path again, he caught up to her, and she felt the weight of him on her back.

She ducked and wriggled away from him, but it was no good. She felt his jaws close on the back of her neck. For a few heartbeats, as she felt his teeth scrape across her skin, she thought that this was the end of her. His jaws would snap shut on her spine and she would die. . . .

But he wasn't holding her like a tiger about to decapitate a mouse. It was more like Peony had once held Rain as a cub, when she'd wandered off and needed to be dragged back home. Except that Sunset wasn't nearly as gentle with his grip: the skin pinched and his teeth drew trickles of blood as he started to drag her along the panda path—*up*, not down.

"Let her go!" Peony roared, and Rain felt Sunset's grip tighten even more as he twitched in pain. She tried to look at what Peony had done, but she couldn't pull herself away without taking a chunk out of the back of her own neck. "Leave my cub alone, you fraud," Peony spat.

"Back off," Sunset snarled, through his mouthful of Rain's fur, "or I'll bite down and finish what I started right here." He bit harder. Rain tried to stop herself, but she couldn't help letting out an involuntary grunt of pain.

Then they were off again, Sunset dragging her along, Rain awkwardly trying to stumble forward on her own paws rather than let him tear the back of her neck any more, his teeth snagging on her skin and his furious breath blowing in her ears. They scrambled up the last few bear-lengths to the top of the hill. Rain caught a blurred glimpse of shocked panda faces before she felt Sunset's muscles bunch, and then she was heaved forward and into the middle of the clearing. She fell awkwardly, striking her shoulder on a stone, and rolled to a stop alone, in the soft grass.

"My fellow pandas," Sunset said, sounding out of breath, as Rain heaved herself dizzily to her paws. "I have found the panda the Dragon warned me of."

Rain looked around. Most of the Prosperhill pandas were there. She could see Azalea, Blossom, Ginseng, Horizon, Fir, and Cypress, Dawn . . . and Pebble. He was staring at her with shock in his wide, liquid eyes. She tried to smile at him. Wasn't he happy she wasn't drowned?

But he kept looking between her ruffled fur, and the blood trickling from her neck, to Sunset behind her. She turned so she could see them both, and noticed Sunset was blocking her way out of the feast clearing as well as Peony's way in.

"I'm alive," she said, turning to her old friends, desperately trying to reclaim control of the situation. "I'm back!"

But it wasn't just Pebble who looked more shocked than happy. She saw Cypress put a paw around Fir and draw her close, the cub's face slowly falling as she picked up on her parents' nervousness.

Rain was surrounded by her friends and family, but she suddenly felt very, very alone.

"Rain . . . ," Pebble said, and Rain turned back to smile at him again, but he still wasn't smiling. In fact, he looked hurt. "So, what was this? Were you just pretending to be dead? Was it all one of your tricks? Where were you?"

"It wasn't a trick!" Rain said hurriedly. "I really was washed away. I tried to get back to you, but I was stuck on the other side of the river. . . ."

"The river receded days ago," said Ginseng.

Rain frowned at him and opened her mouth to explain, but she heard the words in her head and realized they sounded weak. *I was waiting for the right time. . . .*

"I'm sorry for disturbing the peace of the feast clearing," Sunset said, in a measured but sad tone of voice that set Rain's teeth on edge. "You must all hear what Rain has to say. Go on, Rain. Repeat what you said to me."

Rain glared at him. If he wanted her to do it, he must know something she didn't.

But she might never get another opportunity to stand in front of her friends and speak the truth.

"Sunset Deepwood is a fraud," she said. "He's lost his Dragon Speaker powers. Every prophecy he's made since he came to the Prosperhill has been a lie."

She waited for the reaction from the other pandas, and sure enough, she saw several of them sigh and shake their heads.

But she already knew they were sighs of judgment, not surprise. Judgment of *her*.

For a moment she almost felt as if she could see herself as the others saw her: bloodied, untrustworthy, alone, desperate, while Sunset stood proud and powerful and calm behind her.

She wouldn't just give up.

"The reason I was gone is that Sunset Deepwood tried to drown me," she snarled. "He tried to murder me because I found out he was a liar and I confronted him. He's been fooling you all along! He's made a deal with Brawnshanks so the monkeys will fetch striped bamboo for him. He had them beat up Maple!"

"Why would he do that?" Cypress asked, shaking his head. "And *what* striped bamboo?"

"I—I don't know what it was for," Rain admitted. "He drowned me before I could find out!"

"My friends!" Peony shouted, from behind Sunset's shoulder. "If you won't listen to Rain, listen to me! Everything she says is true! I've seen a side of this panda you never have—he is *no* Dragon Speaker!"

Rain saw the heads of several pandas turn toward her, but there was pity in their eyes.

You're my mother, she thought. *Of course you'd believe me—and just like that, he can write off anything you say. He doesn't even have to—they're all doing it for themselves!*

"So it's true," said Blossom evenly. "Just like the prophecy said, Dragon Speaker. *She's* the liar we were waiting for."

"What prophecy?" Rain snarled. "I told you, it's all lies!"

"The Great Dragon spared poor Rain from the river currents," said Sunset, as if she hadn't spoken at all. "And this is how she repays it. This is the liar the Dragon warned me about, and thanks to the Dragon's warning, we were ready for her."

Rain turned to look at Pebble. She knew it was over, but she stared at her friend, willing him to at least look into her eyes. Maybe if he did, he would see that she wasn't lying.

Pebble didn't look at her. He just stared at his paws, pain written across his face.

Rain felt like the Great Dragon itself had wrapped its coils around her and crushed her heart.

"For the good of Prosperhill, Rain and Peony, I rename you *Exile* and banish you from our home. You should leave. We are peaceful pandas here, but we will force you to go if you make us."

Rain kept her gaze fixed on Pebble for a moment longer.

"It's not true," she told him. "Sunset is the liar. I'm sure you'll find out soon enough. Just remember this, will you? Remember that I *tried*."

"Get them out of here," Sunset said, and Blossom and Ginseng stepped forward, putting their large bodies between Rain and Pebble.

Rain glared at Blossom. Blossom looked back with a smug smile on her face that almost made Rain want to fight her, but she knew that it was hopeless.

"I'm going," she said. "Come on, Mother."

"You'll all regret this," said Peony in a low growl, as the pandas closed in and ushered them out of the clearing and down the panda path. "You'll all wish you'd listened to Rain."

Then there was nothing left for Rain and Peony to do but walk, with the sad stares of their friends burning into the fur at the backs of their necks, until the path took them around a corner and out of sight.

Peony stopped as soon as they were hidden from the other

pandas and licked Rain's scratched neck, a little harder than Rain would actually have liked. "I'm so sorry," she said. "My poor cub—look what he did to you. I am still *so* proud of you. I know that you did your best."

"It could have been worse," Rain said. She stopped Peony's frantic grooming and pressed their foreheads together. "We're alive. Let's get away from this horrible place. I didn't want to be a Prosperhill anyway. We can go across the river and find Leaf, just like you said."

Peony nodded shakily. Rain led the way down the path, and as she did, the hatred in her heart for Sunset Deepwood only grew more and more fiery.

Exile. How dare he tell them they were exiled—especially Peony? As far as Rain knew, Peony had rarely been in trouble even as a cub. She'd been popular in the Prosperhill. Now Sunset had turned all her friends against her, and even taken away her name.

He'll pay for this. One way or another. He'll regret that he left us alive....

They trudged toward the Egg Rocks together, Peony's paws dragging with sadness, Rain kicking up leaves in her anger.

Then Rain heard, right above her head, a small sound. In her peripheral vision, something golden ran soundlessly down the trunk of a tree.

"Peony," Rain hissed. "Run!"

Peony looked around in confusion. "What?"

"Run!" Rain shouted, but it was too late. The monkeys

dropped from the branches all around them, more than Rain had seen since that first night she'd watched Sunset and Brawnshanks negotiate their deal. Too many to run from. Too many to fight. Dozens of nimble, gripping paws and lashing golden tails cut them off from any hope of escape.

They were surrounded.

CHAPTER NINETEEN

GHOST STEPPED OUT OF the river and shook himself, staring up at the Northern Forest. Pepper's trail led this way—his fear gave his scent a distinctive edge, and his panic meant he wasn't thinking clearly enough to try to hide it.

Ghost knew exactly which way he'd gone from here—up the nearest slope, breaking twigs and kicking down stones as he went. Even if he hadn't left a scent, Ghost could have tracked him at least that far. He would catch up before Sun Fall, if not sooner.

But then what am I going to do?

He started up the slope, his paws almost seeming to move on their own. He couldn't just go back.

Oh, Shiver. I wish you were here with me. You were right all along.

He let out a growl as he climbed around a patch of mud

where Pepper had slipped and left clear paw marks on the side of the hill.

Sunset's flash of murderous rage had seemed to burn away the version of him Ghost thought he knew—kind, peaceful, concerned only for the safety of the Bamboo Kingdom.

Become the white monster, he'd said.

The echo of Shiver's words seemed to follow him up the slope. *Bloodthirsty, but too stupid to pose a threat.* Now he had no doubt that Sunset had said exactly that.

Was that all he'd seen in Ghost from the start? A predator who could be used, pointed at anyone Sunset wanted to intimidate? That was all his special missions were, after all—an attempt to intimidate the monkeys, and then Pepper. He'd wanted him to search for triplets in the Northern Forest so he could drag them back to the Prosperhill and interrogate them, too—and instead they'd found Plum.

You're a fraud, she'd said.

She wasn't crazy at all.

And she had attacked first, but Sunset hadn't hesitated to sink his claws into her. . . .

Ghost stumbled to a halt on the crest of the hill.

I knew, he thought. *I knew it wasn't a tiger that killed her. But I didn't see what was staring me right in the face. She wasn't killed by a predator at all.*

He turned and looked back across the river, at the Prosperhill with its rippling slopes dotted with bright bamboo, and a few distant black-and-white shapes walking or resting on the hillsides.

Sunset Deepwood is a liar and a murderer.

And I was so blind to it, I even drove my own sister away.

Would he ever see Shiver again? Would he ever be able to tell her how sorry he was, how stupid he'd been?

And what was he going to do about it now?

Pepper's scent ran along the crest of this hill and up into a patch of long grass. With a deep sigh, Ghost followed the trail. Pepper had left a path of crushed grass behind him. On the other side of it, the fear in his scent seemed to dim, as if he thought once he'd gotten this far that they wouldn't be able to chase him.

But Ghost had learned to hunt from the best hunter in the White Spine Mountains. He tried not to think about what Winter would say if she were here, and instead focused on following Pepper up the hill and down into a small valley on the other side, then along, downriver but always hidden from the water and the Southern Forest. The snapped twigs and muddy paw prints were easy enough to spot.

Finally Ghost looked up and saw a black-and-white shape moving on the slope above him. Ghost held his breath and hunkered down behind a clump of ferns, but Pepper didn't look around. He was sniffing at some bamboo canes, and as Ghost watched, he flopped down beside them and started to pull off the leaves.

He really had no idea he was still being followed. In fact, Pepper had that distinctive look of carefree happiness on his face that had frustrated and confused Ghost. It still confused him. But watching Pepper now, chewing on the bamboo leaves as if he'd never even met Sunset, let alone nearly been murdered by him, he felt the confusion bring a kind of clarity.

He's an idiot. Or at least he really doesn't think that anything can hurt him. He got away from Sunset, so now everything must be fine. . . .

Ghost was surprised to find himself feeling a little jealous. It must be nice to walk through the world feeling like you could do absolutely anything you liked and it would all work out in the end.

He watched while Pepper finished eating and got up again. He sniffed around for a while and then wandered into a small dip in the hill, which deepened and turned into a narrow ditch running up toward the top of the slope, ending in a cave.

Ghost shook his head. It was the perfect place for an ambush, and if he were Pepper—well, he wouldn't be in this situation to start with, but he wouldn't have gone into that ditch for all the bamboo in the Southern Forest.

He followed, keeping his paw steps as silent as he could as he gained more and more ground on the wandering panda. Ghost stayed up on the side of the ditch and tracked Pepper almost all the way to the cave at the top, without Pepper ever looking around and seeing or scenting him.

Then he dropped down into the ditch, sliding down the steep side and landing on the path, between Pepper and any hope of escape.

Pepper heard the noise and turned, and then fell onto his haunches with a yelp.

"Ghost!" he whined. "Don't—wait, please—" He backed up and then threw himself at the wall of the ditch, trying to scramble out. But it was too steep, and Ghost was on him in a few strides and bearing him to the floor, paws pinning him on his belly.

"Stay down," Ghost snarled.

Pepper yelled and wriggled, but Ghost was stronger. Pepper was like any other prey—he was panicking, trying to bite and claw at Ghost but only getting in a slight scratch on his foreleg, which Ghost ignored.

"Please let me go! I'm sorry," Pepper babbled. "I didn't mean it about Sunset—I'm sure he's not a liar—I just say things. I thought it would be funny! I'm not even really a triplet—I'm nobody—I just said that. Please don't kill me!"

"Funny?" Ghost shook his head and growled in Pepper's ear. "None of this is *funny*. I don't give a monkey's tail if you're a triplet. I don't trust you. You're a liar and you're dangerous. Are you listening to me? Just nod."

Pepper nodded so hard he left a groove in the mud under his face.

"If you want to live, stay away from the Southern Forest. *Far* away, *forever*. Do you understand? You can never, ever go back there. You leave here, and you keep walking, or we're going to have a problem, and you won't be able to wriggle out of it this time. *Do you understand?*"

"Yes!" Pepper squeaked.

Ghost sighed and stepped back. Pepper wriggled to his paws and stood for a second, staring at Ghost, as if he couldn't believe his luck. Then he edged around Ghost and broke into a run, slipping and sliding back down the ditch.

Ghost watched him reach the bottom, turn downstream, and pound away into the bushes as fast as his paws would take him.

Did I do the right thing? Ghost wondered. *Whatever trouble he's up to, now he's out there and free to cause as much harm as he likes. . . .*

But what else could he do? He wouldn't kill another panda, not for Sunset Deepwood.

Shiver would agree he'd done the right thing.

With heavy paws and a deep, unsettled feeling in his chest, he set off on the long walk back to the Southern Forest.

Before he crossed over the river, Ghost stopped and looked back.

What if he just didn't go back to the Prosperhill? What if he left these pandas, who mostly didn't even like him, to deal with Sunset on their own? What if he headed back to the mountains after all? Perhaps he could try to catch up with Shiver. . . .

But that was a fantasy. The reality was that Sunset was a killer, and only Ghost knew it. Could he really abandon the Prosperhill, where he'd briefly felt at home for the first time in his life?

No. I'm not sure what I'm going to do, but I can't just leave.

If he was going to stay, he should make sure Sunset didn't suspect anything.

He bent his head and chewed at the place on his leg where

Pepper had scratched him. The blood was drying, but he managed to smear it across his muzzle. Then he padded over the river crossing and up the panda path.

Something was wrong—he could sense it as soon as he stepped into the feast clearing. The pandas huddled in small groups, talking urgently in low voices. Sunset was sitting at the base of the tree where he sometimes gave prophecies, hunched over as if he was exhausted. It didn't feel like this was all still a reaction to Plum's death. Something else had happened.

The closest pandas turned and saw Ghost. One of them was Pebble. He actively recoiled from Ghost's bloodied muzzle, tripped over his own paw, and sat down heavily on his haunches. He looked as frightened as Pepper had been.

"What happened?" murmured Mist. "What did you do?"

Ghost hesitated. Should he just *tell* her what Sunset had told him to do? But Sunset could just deny it, and who would these pandas believe? Not the outsider freak.

Sunset was on his paws now and hurrying over to him.

"Step back, all of you," he said. The pandas did, stumbling away from Ghost. They seemed relieved to be able to put a few bear-lengths between him and them. "I must speak to Ghost alone."

Ghost simply nodded, and followed Sunset out of the clearing. They didn't go far, just far enough down the path not to be overheard.

"I found Pepper," Ghost said. He looked up into Sunset's face. He couldn't believe he'd thought the big panda was his friend. "I killed him. That's what you wanted, isn't it?"

Sunset's eyes glinted. "Yes," he said.

He admitted it. Ghost felt the fur all down his back prickle and stand on end. He felt like he was standing on a teetering rock at the top of a cliff, exhilarated and terrified all at once.

"You've done so well," Sunset said, and stepped forward to press his forehead to Ghost's. With a great effort, Ghost didn't flinch away. "You've proved yourself to be the most loyal ally I could ever wish for. You have my thanks, and the gratitude of the whole Bamboo Kingdom. I wish I could say our work is over—but I have another task for you now."

Ghost nodded, only half listening to Sunset's platitudes. Up above him, he could see movement as a couple of black-and-white faces peered over the lip of the rock surrounding the feast clearing. They couldn't hear Sunset, but they were watching him and whispering to each other. He could guess what they were saying.

Why does Ghost have blood on his muzzle? Whose is it? Is it Pepper's? Did that monster kill that poor cub?

Ghost looked down at his white paws and sighed. None of them would trust him again. He was the only one who knew about Sunset's treachery, and it would stay that way until he could figure out a way to prove it to them.

I really am all alone now.

CHAPTER TWENTY

"I CAN'T BELIEVE WE found them," Leaf panted. She sat down on the edge of the ditch, watching the mouth of the cave from above. The ditch was a crack in the ground that ran all the way up a steep slope, getting deeper as it went, until at the end it met a rocky cave in the peak of the hill.

Inside, she could hear the squeaking and rustling of hundreds of tiny bats.

"My paws ache," said Dasher, flopping down in the leaves beside her. "I hope they take a good long rest before they set off again!"

"Me too," said Leaf, stretching.

"I think I can smell pandas," Dasher said, his long tail twitching. "Can you smell that?"

Leaf sniffed the ground at her feet, then the ditch, and then the sky, tasting the air all around her.

"I think I can too! But I mostly smell bats right now," she added. "But maybe the other triplet has been this way. Maybe we're close?"

"I hope so," said Dasher, rolling over and stretching, waving his paws in the air and then curling them in to his chest.

Leaf watched the cave, her heart beating steady and strong. She did wish that the bats would let them rest for a while before they went on with their chase, but she also felt a strange longing building up in her chest, an almost unbearable weight of hope.

Could we really be close? she thought. *Could we actually be about to meet my other sibling? What will they be like?*

Shapes moved in the cave, and then all at once the bats were out, zipping through the air around Leaf's head, a few at a time at first and then more and more of them. Leaf got to her paws and stretched.

"Come on," she said. "Better get ready. Once they've fed, it'll be time to go."

But this time, something different was happening.

The bats were returning to the cave . . . and staying there.

They streamed out in ones and two, flying in all directions, but they always came back to the cave.

Leaf's heart began to race.

"They're not leaving," Dasher said.

"This is it," whispered Leaf. "Dash, this is *it*! This is where they live—it's where they were leading us all the time!"

"Are you sure?" Dasher peered into the darkness.

Leaf took a deep breath, then slid over the edge of the ditch to the bottom and padded toward the mouth of the cave. A wriggling mass of tiny bodies clung to the roof of it, eating the insects they'd caught or wrapping themselves in their wings again to settle down to sleep.

"Are they here?" Leaf called up to them. "Is the triplet here?"

The bats began to speak again, in their chattering, high-pitched voices. But now, Leaf found that in all the hubbub, she could make out a word, repeated over and over again.

"Here! Is here! Was here! Here, here, here!"

"Thank you!" Leaf cried. She turned to shout up to Dasher on the edge of the ditch. "Let's look around! Try to find that panda scent!"

"Right!" Dasher chirped, and turned away.

"Oh, and remember!" Leaf called after him. "If you meet one, before you do anything else, check for the white grip pad! It should look just like mine."

"Gotcha," said Dasher, with a flick of his long tail.

Leaf sniffed around the ditch. There was definitely a scent here, and she even found a few white hairs sticking out of the mud. But the scent seemed both quite recent and slightly confused. Had there been one panda here, or several? What if it was just a group of normal pandas, and not her triplet at all? If they had been here, and then they'd moved on, why would they come back? If there was a panda trail to follow, should they follow it? But she didn't want to go too far from the bats. They'd said *here*. . . .

She got to the bottom of the ditch and met Dasher, who was scratching behind his ear.

"Panda scents go in more than one direction from here," he said. "One into those bushes, and one down that valley, and there might be more."

"Should we check the cave itself again? I didn't actually go in," Leaf muttered.

Dasher made an uncertain noise. "You mean go inside, with the bats?"

"They won't hurt you," Leaf said, prodding Dasher with her nose and turning to go back up the slope. "You're a bit bigger than they can carry!"

Dasher made another *hmmm* noise, and dragged a little way behind Leaf as she hurried up the bottom of the ditch toward the cave mouth. As she approached, she realized that Sun Fall had passed, and the hillside was distinctly darker than it had been when they arrived. The inside of the cave was completely black after a few bear-lengths, and she couldn't clearly make out the bats anymore, except for the ones closest to the entrance.

She swallowed and stepped inside.

"I don't like the thing their wings do, is all," Dasher muttered behind her. "Anyway, what about the white monster that attacked Plum? *That* happened in a cave."

"A long way away from here," Leaf reminded him. "I'm going in to look."

"I'll stand guard out here," said Dasher.

Leaf rolled her eyes and stepped farther into the cave.

It went back a long way farther than she'd been expecting. Rocks stuck up from the ground around her, and her paws splashed suddenly into cold water. There was a small, dark pond here that must overflow when it rained and run off down the ditch. The smell and sound of bats was all around her.

But there was no sign of another panda.

"Do we have this wrong somehow?" Leaf asked, emerging from the cave. Dasher startled, and then shook his head fiercely.

"No. After they led us all the way to the Darkpool pandas and then here? No. You're a Dragon Speaker, and the bats are helping you. We'll work this out."

Leaf smiled at him and nuzzled the back of his head with her nose. "I'm so glad you're with me, Dash."

"I'm very helpful, it's true," Dasher said smugly. "You sit here in case the triplet comes back; I'll go find some bamboo for the Feast of Moon Climb. That'll cheer you up. And everything always seems clearer after a nap."

Leaf sat and looked up at the sky as Dasher scampered off down the ditch. The clouds were swirling above, with peeks of deep blue and scattered stars winking at her and then vanishing again.

Great Dragon, she thought. *I know you will guide me to where I need to be. Please do the same for both my siblings. If I'm to meet my triplet here, so be it. If not, please show them the path they need to walk.*

She looked down, pleased with how she'd put her request. It was the right thing to say. It wasn't for her to decide where they were needed.

Then she looked up again.

But I'd really like to meet them, if it's not too much trouble.

Leaf woke up with a start and looked around, for a moment not quite remembering where she was. Then it all came back to her—she was in the cave, her paws resting on hard, cool stone. The bats above her were fast asleep, the occasional whiffle of tiny bat snores echoing through the cavern. Dasher was curled up beside her, the remains of their Moon Climb and Moon Fall feasts nearby.

It was light outside the cave, the dazzling light of a new dawn shining on one side of the cave entrance. They must have slept through the Feast of Gray Light altogether. The light was so bright that when she looked out of the cave she had to blink to see what was right in front of her.

There was a shape there.

Leaf leaped to her paws.

Dasher startled awake beside her. "Hmm, what?"

"There's something here!" Leaf hissed. Cautiously, still blinking in the bright Golden Light, she stepped out of the cave.

The shape outside was a young panda. He was sniffing cautiously at the cave mouth, and jumped back when he saw Leaf.

She noticed he seemed to favor one front paw, not seeming to want to put the other down on the ground.

Could it be . . . ?

"Hello," she said. "Sorry if I startled you! We were sleeping in the cave."

Dasher padded toward the panda, who had sat down again now, still holding his paw awkwardly in front of him.

"Hi. My name's Pepper," he said. "This is going to sound a bit strange, but . . . I think the Great Dragon brought me here. Do you know anything about . . . why?"

Leaf thought her heart was going to rattle right out of her chest, and Dasher was looking from her to Pepper and back again with an astonished grin on his small face. But she had to keep a cool head. She had to be sure.

"Did something happen to your paw?" she asked. "Can I see?"

Pepper held out his paw, and Leaf's body jolted in shock. His grip pad wasn't white, but it wasn't black or gray, either—it was bloody and red, a new scab forming over a nasty-looking wound right across it.

"I had to do it," Pepper said. Leaf realized he was shaking. "The monkeys were after me. The ones with the blue faces. They were looking for the cub with the white grip pad, so I—I decided to hide it."

"Pepper . . . ," Leaf breathed. She couldn't hold it back any longer. She ran over to him and nuzzled his cheek gently. "I'm so sorry that happened to you," she said. "But it's going to be all right now. My name's Leaf, and I think I'm your sister!"

"You're . . . you're one of the triplets?" Pepper gasped. He nuzzled her back. "I've looked for you for so long! I'm so happy I found you! Have you seen the other one? Do you know what's going on? All I know is I was lost and alone and then the monkeys found me and I didn't know what to do. . . ."

"Yes, I've met our sister!" Leaf found herself almost hopping with joy, pacing back and forth in front of her new brother, her heart overflowing with everything she needed to tell him. "She's called Rain! And . . . well, I do know what's going on, sort of, but you should probably brace yourself for this." She made herself sit down again to deliver the news face-to-face. "The reason we're special, the reason we survived and the Great Dragon is helping us find each other . . . is that we're the next Dragon Speakers. All three of us together. Oh, by the Nine Feasts I'm so glad I found you!" She nuzzled Pepper again and gave him a hard lick between the eyes.

For a moment, Pepper looked overwhelmed, even slightly uncertain.

"This is . . . more than I expected," he said. "It's a lot to take in, but . . . I'm glad I found you too! My new sister!" He brightened as he looked up at Leaf.

"And I'm Dasher Climbing Far," Dasher piped up. Leaf laughed, and shifted to let Dasher sit beside her.

"He's my best friend," she said. "He helped me find you too!" She looked up at the sky, which blazed blue and pink as the sun rose over the Bamboo Kingdom. She felt as if all the hopes she'd barely dared to hope were coming true all at once. "Now we just need to find Rain and make our way back to the Dragon Mountain."

"And then what?" Pepper asked excitedly.

Leaf grinned at him. "Then we fulfill our destiny. Then we become what we were born to be. All three of us, together."

CHAPTER TWENTY-ONE

". . . NOW!" RAIN YELLED, and broke into a run. She didn't have time to look back and check whether Peony was running too. They had to hold to the plan. She managed to knock a couple of monkeys flying, even treading on one as she ran. It let out a satisfying squeak of annoyance. Then Rain was off and running, heading for the undergrowth—

Something landed on her back, and then all she could see was golden bodies and angry blue faces. Monkeys grabbed pawfuls of her fur and threw their arms around her legs. She stumbled to a stop, rearing and growling. She tried to shake them off, but there were just too many. One of them sank its sharp teeth into her ear, and she yelped as she felt the skin split and blood trickle down into her fur.

The monkey laughed. "Did you think it would be that easy? Back on the path!"

Two monkeys dropped down on the path in front of her, shrieking and snapping and flailing their long arms at her, trying to get her to back up.

I could fight, she thought.

But if she did, she wouldn't be able to hold back. Even if she could get away without their sharp claws finding her eyes or their teeth finding her throat, she would have to kill them to do it. Lots of them.

She backed up. Slowly the weight of grasping monkeys on her lessened, until she was walking with only one clinging to her back, its breath rasping near her ear.

She turned around and saw that Peony hadn't even gotten as far as she had—she was still sitting on the path, growling at a ring of golden monkeys that had her completely surrounded.

"Where are we going?" Rain demanded, as the monkeys prodded her back onto the path.

The one on her back sniggered. "You'll soon find out," he said.

They were herded to the edge of the Prosperhill, monkeys snapping at their paws and swinging from the branches overhead, ready to drop down on them if they made another attempt to escape. Peony glanced at Rain, and Rain shook her head.

It was useless to try again. They should wait until they knew what Sunset planned to do with them.

She hoped that was the right choice.

She tried to guess where they were going as they

walked—Rain had ranged pretty far around the Prosperhill, but she had no way to tell how much farther the monkeys would march them, or what for.

When they finally reached their destination, Rain stopped in her tracks. She'd seen this clearing before, but the last time she was here, it hadn't had a large open pit right in the center of it.

Another golden monkey was waiting for them, sitting on the edge of the pit with one leg dangling. It was Brawnshanks. He hopped up onto his haunches when he saw them approach, and gave them a sweeping bow that took in both pandas and the edge of the pit.

"In you go," he said.

"No," Peony breathed. She shot Rain a frightened look.

"You can't make us go in there," Rain growled at Brawnshanks, stepping in front of Peony. But she knew it was an empty protest. The monkey on her back dug its claws into her shoulders, and she roared and shook it off, but as soon as it thumped into the leaves, another three were on her. The rest advanced, jabbing and biting, driving her toward the edge. She stood her ground, spinning around to swipe at the monkeys, and she even seized one by its twitching tail and threw it into the bushes. But she was still giving ground.

Behind her, she heard Peony yell, and a sound of scrambling and then a thump.

"Mother!" Rain turned and ran to the edge of the pit and looked down.

The pit was deep, more than three bear-lengths, and the sides were nearly sheer mud and rocks. Peony lay at the bottom. Rain's breath caught and then released as her mother stirred and sat up, looking mostly unharmed, but her eyes full of shock.

Rain glanced over her shoulder at the monkeys hopping toward her, and made a decision. She wasn't going to let them tip her in face-first, like a cub playing with a pine cone.

She turned around and let herself down into the pit, back legs first, sliding down the wall with as much dignity as she could muster. Her back foot struck a rock sticking out from the side of the pit and she landed awkwardly on it. She tried to ignore the pain, and stared up defiantly at the blue faces of the monkeys as they peered over the edge.

The laughter of Brawnshanks and his troop echoed through the clearing and seemed to fill the pit.

Rain turned away.

"Are you all right?" she asked Peony.

"Bruised," said Peony. "Nothing broken. But what are we going to do? Can you climb out of here?"

"No," Rain said. "I think even Leaf would struggle to get back up there, especially if those monkeys are going to hang around to try to stop us."

"Maybe they'll leave," Peony whispered. "And we can try to dig our way out?"

"Yeah. Maybe," Rain said.

But she didn't feel very hopeful. The pit had looked huge

from above—it was big enough for both pandas to lie down in—but down here the walls seemed to close in over her head. Her world shrank to mud and stone and Peony and the jeering faces of the troop, and there was nothing she could do about it. The anger that had gotten her through so much, ever since Sunset's return to the forest, seemed to seep away into the mud at her paws.

For what felt like an incredibly long time, nothing more happened. The monkeys grew bored of pointing and laughing at the two pandas, and their heads vanished, but Rain could still hear them chattering and jeering and arguing among themselves up above. Peony gave a shudder, and Rain tried not to think about how cold it would be here in the middle of the night, or whether the monkeys would feed them, or what would happen when it rained. . . .

Then suddenly the tone of the monkeys' chatter changed. Rain and Peony looked up, and saw two panda faces reach the edge of the pit and look down at them.

It was Sunset and the white monster. The white panda looked strangely emotionless, but Sunset was smirking. The sight was enough to rekindle the anger in Rain's heart.

"What now?" she yelled up. "What are you going to do with us now?"

"I'm sure you can imagine that for yourself," Sunset sneered. "You have *many* potential uses. Of course, I can't say the same for Peony. So you had better behave yourself, hadn't you? Or I might decide that I don't need her alive."

Rain took a breath to curse at him, but Peony caught her eye and shook her head. Rain simply growled.

"Rain, this is my friend Ghost," Sunset said. "I don't believe you've met."

"I've heard of him," Rain snarled. The white panda blinked impassively.

"Ghost is a loyal panda, but he was trained to hunt and kill by the fierce snow leopards of the White Spine Mountains," Sunset said. "He will make sure that you stay exactly where you've been put. Enjoy your new home. You will be here for some time."

Before Rain could think of a retort, Sunset was gone, leaving Ghost alone, staring down into the pit.

Rain glared up at him.

"*You*," she said. "You're the white monster that attacked Plum. And now this. Doing Sunset's dirty work for him. Plum was right the first time. You're no panda—you really are a monster."

Ghost's brows drew into an angry frown, and his shoulders hunched as he took a breath, as if he was going to say something. But then he just turned away too. Rain growled after him. He didn't even have anything to say in his own defense. *Monster.*

Rain stayed still, staring up into the sky, for a little while. But it seemed that now, except for a few lingering monkey voices, they really had been left alone.

Peony slumped against a rock, hanging her head.

"We're going to get out of here," Rain said.

"Of course," Peony said, looking up and brightening, though Rain was pretty sure she was faking her cheer for Rain's sake—she sounded just like she always had when Rain had been a little cub and told her one day she would swim across the river and back. "Of course we will. If anyone can find a way out of here, it's you."

Rain sighed, and curled up close beside her. "Obviously," she said.

But it's not obvious at all. I can't do this alone—I need help.

And I'm not sure even the Great Dragon can help us now.

EPILOGUE

SHIVER LAY PERFECTLY STILL underneath the ferns, not a twitch of her tail or a flick of a whisker to give her away to the golden monkeys that surrounded the pit in the clearing—or to her brother.

Oh, Ghost, she thought. *What in the Snow Cat's name have you gotten yourself into?*

She had gone as far as the river before turning back. She couldn't go back to the mountains and leave Ghost here, with these pandas who were just using him, even though he was acting like he had fur for brains. She'd been watching him ever since, carefully dodging the other bears and Sunset's troop of monkeys.

Once, she had chosen a hiding place near the panda path and found a panda already hiding there. That had been Rain.

Lurking nearby, she'd gathered that Rain wasn't on Sunset's side either. She hadn't seen what happened when Rain went up to the feast clearing with Peony and Sunset, but Rain and Peony were now down in the pit she'd seen Blossom and Ginseng digging one night, so she guessed it couldn't have gone well.

Now Ghost was sitting near the pit, his head hanging miserably. As she watched, he lay down on his belly, his chin resting on the ground, and closed his eyes with a deep sigh.

Shiver longed to talk to him. She was sure he would listen to her now. She didn't know what was going on with him, but it was clear he didn't want to be here, keeping these two pandas down in that hole.

Unfortunately, it was also pretty clear that Sunset was too clever to leave Ghost completely alone with his prisoners. There were still monkeys on guard around the pit, including Brawnshanks, their burly leader, and several others.

One of them, sitting on the opposite side of the pit from Ghost, picked up a piece of rotting yellow gingko fruit, tossed it from paw to paw, and then lobbed it down into the pit. Shiver heard a splat and a string of panda growls from inside the pit, and the monkey fell onto her back, screeching with laughter. Brawnshanks laughed too. So did all the monkeys—except one smaller one, who walked up to the one who'd thrown the gingko fruit and shoved her over onto her front.

"Stop it, Jitterpaws," she said. "That's not right! We're guards, not torturers."

Jitterpaws hopped to her feet and looked like she was about to smack the younger female, but then Brawnshanks stepped between them. Instead of reprimanding Jitterpaws, though, he drew himself up and towered over the younger one, his blue face splitting in a grin that showed all his pointed teeth.

"Once again the noble Nimbletail has something to teach us," he said, his voice oily and menacing. "Do you want to go down in the pit too, Nimbletail?"

"No," Nimbletail said. There was an edge of defiance in her voice, but then she stepped back and pressed her belly to the ground in front of her leader. "Sorry, Brawnshanks. But the Dragon Speaker did say not to hurt his prisoners *too* much, right?"

Brawnshanks laughed.

"Sunset Deepwood may *think* they're his prisoners, that doesn't make it true. *I'm* the one in charge here."

"Right!" said Jitterpaws, prodding Nimbletail hard in the chest with one long finger. "The monkeys rule this forest, no matter what the big stupid bears think. Maybe one day soon your 'Dragon Speaker' will go down in the pit with them!"

Brawnshanks chortled, but then turned and grabbed Jitterpaws's face with one hand.

"Shh! Careful the white cub doesn't hear you," he hissed.

Shiver shuddered, her fur rippling down her back. Her gaze was drawn back to Ghost. He hadn't moved.

I think you're in even more trouble than you know, she thought. *But don't worry! I'm going to help you, no matter what.*

She looked up, through the ferns, to the darkening sky above. She couldn't see the stars, but she imagined them, shining bright just as they would have in the sky over the White Spine Mountains.

Snow Cat, hear me—I promise to you that I'll help my brother, and the captured pandas too, even if they don't believe in you.

She looked down again, and her eyes rested on the young monkey, Nimbletail, who had walked away from the others and was sitting alone, picking at her tail with a worried look on her face.

And I think I know just where to start. . . .